D0246890

000002171189

Gunfight at the Nameless Village

Harry James Luck, Civil War veteran, US Cavalry captain, sometime lawman, gambler and part-time town drunk, resigns his army commission and heads south to the High Plains country of Texas in the hope of settling down to a trouble and conflict-free life. He meets the lovely Bonnie Luxford, buys a small but attractive ranch and sees his trail clear ahead and going on forever.

Texas trails never run straight, though, and a wandering band of Comancheros bring the dream to a fire-ravaged close. Harry knows he cannot forever hide in a bottle and with an elderly Comanche as his only companion, he sets his sights on a new road, a trail of revenge. The two men, together with a small company of adventurous young Texas Rangers and an over-the-hill lawman, seek out the infamous Comanchero Miguel Sanchez and beard him in his own den, a little Mexican hamlet without a name. What followed went down in Western folklore as the Gunfight at the Nameless Village.

By the same author

The Shadow Rider
Shadow on a Dark Mountain
Ride a Long Shadow
Shadow of the Apache
A Man Called Crow

Writing as Harry Jay Thorn
Hard Ride to Primrose
Incident at Laughing Water Creek
Wyoming Payday Saturday Night
The Sweetwater Kill
The Far Side of the River
Long Ride to Serenity
Hard Ride to Glory
The Vineyards of Hell
The Dark Trail to Nowhere
Where no Ravens Fly

Gunfight at the Nameless Village

Chris Adam Smith

ROBERT HALE

© Chris Adam Smith 2018
First published in Great Britain 2018

ISBN 978-0-7198-2719-8

The Crowood Press
The Stable Block
Crowood Lane
Ramsbury
Marlborough
Wiltshire SN8 2HR

www.bhwesterns.com

Robert Hale is an imprint
of The Crowood Press

The right of Chris Adam Smith to be identified as
author of this work has been asserted by him
in accordance with the Copyright, Designs and
Patents Act 1988

All rights reserved. No part of this publication may be
reproduced or transmitted in any form or by any means,
electronic or mechanical, including photocopying, recording,
or any information storage and retrieval system, without
permission in writing from the publishers.

Toby ... *always.*

DUDLEY LIBRARIES

000002171189

Askews & Holts | 31-May-2018
£14.50
2CO

PROLOGUE

The thin scarecrow of a man stumbled along the sidewalk, his pathway lit by a long row of kerosene lamps guttering in the cold, autumn breeze, his laboured breath turning to white vapour. It was a bad night, the shadows had him by the throat and he desperately needed a drink, and the Lucky Black Cat was the nearest saloon on the northern side of the tracks that would likely tolerate his presence. His grey town suit was crusted with dirt and horse shit from his livery stable bed, the only resting place open to him on the nights he needed shelter. His shirt was sweat-stained, stiff and grubby, his once highly-polished boots were down at heel, dull and had long since given up any pretence of keeping out the rain. His narrow, weather-beaten face had not seen a razor in a long while and a stale odour clung to the air with his every passing step. There was a sweat-stained battered Stetson on his head, leaking dark, matted hair, the front of the brim turned upwards as if he were constantly walking into a brisk wind, two small holes denoting the one-time presence of an insignia of some kind. He had a quarter of a dollar in his clenched, shaking fist, two bits he had mooched off a drummer who thought the money well worth his departure.

There were two customers bellied up to the bar, one, a tall, severe-looking man in a black hat, pants and a dark frock coat. He had pale-blue eyes surrounded by deep crow's feet, a narrow mouth and his sombre, tanned face was broken by the long, neatly-trimmed, drooping, grey moustache. The other customer was a young cowhand in well-worn but serviceable range-clothes, one of the many drovers passing through Canterville hoping to find work, having spent their return fare home to Texas on some of the more dubious delights, both sides of the Canterville railroad tracks had to offer. He wore a sidearm high on his left hip, grips forward.

The thin man settled himself at the bar between the two customers and laid his coin on the bar. 'Whiskey and chaser please, Henry.' He focused on the tall man in the long bar mirror and nodded. The man nodded back but did not return the weak smile offered. The barkeep poured him a whiskey, drew a frothing pint and scooped the foam off with a wooden spatula before placing it on the bar. The man's shaking hand quickly wrapped itself around the glass, the cool beer washing down the harsh spirit.

'Jesus H, you stink.' The youngster turned to the tired man.

'I'm sorry,' he said, and moved a little way along the bar.

'Sorry don't get it half done, old man.' There was a mean edge to the youngster's voice. 'Get the hell out of here before I kick your skinny ass out on to the street, you Goddamned rummy.'

'I'll just finish my drink and I will be on my way.'

'You will be on your damned way right now.' He swung a loose hand at the man, knocking the glass from his shaking grip. 'I said right now.'

'Stay hard, Harry.' The big man in black moved to face the pair. 'You, kid, you buy the man a drink and then move on. I suggest you might find more affable company in one of the Mex joints on the other side of the tracks. You don't belong here, that's plain to see.' His voice was deep, tobacco stained, a little above a whisper, compelling, a lived-in voice you listened to.

'And who the hell might you be? Another rummy?'

'I won't tell you again, son.' The man let his long coat open, the holstered Colt on his left hip and a five-pointed nickel-plated star on the left side of his grey vest.

'They elect you to protect scum like this?' the

young cowboy asked, and nodded in the direction of the tired man who stood very still, staring dismally at the spilled beer and broken glass on the sawdust covered floor.

'They elected me to serve and protect. They do not tell me who to serve and protect, I just know. Now you put two bits on the bar and be gone from my sight before I am tempted to put you in the ground. Texas dirt is hard to dig this time of the year and it is not something I would choose to do.' He paused. 'Do you get my meaning here, sonny?' The threat in the slowly delivered words was very real and palpable.

The cowboy dug a quarter out of his pants pocket and slammed it on the bar, turned on his heel and smashed his way through double doors that sheltered the batwings in winter.

'You didn't have to do that, George. He was right, I am pretty ripe. I could have gone, should have gone.'

The sheriff moved to the man's side and laid a silver dollar on the bar. 'Give Harry his drink, Henry, then take him out back and get him a hot bath and a change of clothes, if you have any traveller's left-behinds.'

'I don't need no hot bath, George. I'll go down to the creek first thing in the morning.'

'Harry, the creek is damned near froze over. You get a hot bath and come down to the jail. You can sleep in one of the cells and maybe do a few chores for me in the morning, but this nonsense has to end now, right here this very night.' He pushed the silver dollar forward to the bartender. 'Get him a hot bath, Henry, and any spare clothing you can find, then see to it that he comes along to my office directly.'

Henry nodded.

The sheriff turned back to the tired man. 'I mean it, Harry, this has to end here. You must move on. Yesterday is dead and gone and there is no going back. For all our sakes, it has to end here.'

The man nodded, his hands had stilled a little and he finished the fresh schooner of beer.

'I got some clothes that should fit you, Harry, not new but clean and left here by one of the Texican drovers, so they do have some pedigree.' Henry offered a smile and lifted the bar-flap, signalling the man through. 'I'll get the Chinaman to get the water hot for you and I'll bring you a toddy when you are in but, like George said, it has to end here.'

The man nodded then turned and smiled a crooked smile at the sheriff. 'Thanks, George, I understand, I won't be any more trouble. Guess I will be moving on come first light.'

'No need for that, my friend. We are all here for you.'

The man followed Henry through to the bathhouse in the rear of the big storeroom and standing in the open glow of the potbellied stove, began to strip his filthy clothes, leaving them in a ragged pile around his naked, narrow, burn-scarred body.

Henry said, 'Around five eleven I guess, you need to put some weight back on though. Get some of that grey cut out of your hair, a shave and your moustache trimmed short like it used to be. I can take care of the clothes and the Chinaman can take care of the rest.'

'You think he would have pulled on that kid, Henry, even killed him maybe?'

'Yes, I believe he would have if you were in danger.'

'He really cares that much?'

'We all do, Harry, we all do.'

'I'm keeping the hat.'

'Whatever you say, Harry, whatever you say.'

That was the first day of the rest of my life. I was a drunk, a one-time peace-officer and US Army captain riding with the Sixth Cavalry out of Fort Laramie, a failed man. My name is Harry James Luck and most people call me Harry or HJ and this is my story. . . .

CHAPTER ONE

ON THE RISE

I mustered out of Fort Laramie on a cold autumn morning in 1877, twelve years after the end of the Civil War. The sky was a leaden grey and there was a smell of rain, or worse, early snow on the wind. I could have lingered but I had had enough of the US Army and its Washington-instigated brutal treatment of the Native American population, destroying a way of life, a whole people gone in a money-grubbing steal for gold and land. The savage and unnecessary slaying of Crazy Horse of the Oglala Lakota people at Fort Robinson in Nebraska was just about the last straw for me and I immediately resigned my commission as a captain of the 6th Cavalry and headed west on a semi-retired chestnut named as Blaze on the bill of sale;

my army pants, boots and hat, with the insignia removed, a red shirt in place of the bibbed dirty shirt blue and a long, second-hand, sheepskin jacket purchased at the Suttler's Store. I bought a western saddle to replace the McClellan I had grown so accustomed to pounding my backside numb on seemingly endless patrols. I also swapped my flapped holster and Sam Brown for a plain, black-leather shell belt and high-ride holster for my .44.40 Colt Army with its seven-and-a-half-inch barrel which, in keeping with the tradition of the officer corps, was of my own purchase and honed to my own specification by the Fort Laramie gunsmith. Similarly, I purchased a Winchester Rifle and handed in my issued Henry, the former using the same ammunition as the handgun; seemed like a worthwhile expense.

I had no real destination in mind. West seemed the way to go and I had a fair-sized poke in my saddle-bag and money in the Wells Fargo Bank at Laramie, saved army pay and a penchant for poker had boosted that considerably. I was in no hurry and certainly not looking for work but seeking a haven, a place to put down some roots. I was all army, an army brat, born and bred. My father, a major in the Union Army, was taken by a Confederate Minie ball when I was sixteen years old and I enlisted shortly after the death of my mother that following spring. I had grown up with the US Army and leaving left me rudderless and somewhat adrift in a sea of uncertainty.

My best prospect seemed to be in ranching as the search for gold was of no interest to me whatsoever. Texas appeared to be the direction to head so, crossing Colorado and the north-east corner of New Mexico, I reckoned would be around some four-hundred miles and a gentle month's riding. Also, heading southeast would lessen the chance of running into any of the bitter, wintry weather soon to be blowing down from the distant Rocky Mountains, leaving that threat well behind me on the northern plains. Cold is not a climate of which I am overly fond.

Texas, it was rumoured, was a good place for a man to get himself lost. It was not fully settled and there was good land to be had for a man with money to spend. Reconstruction had been poorly handled in parts of the state, but in others the war had made very little impact. Texans are very much for Texas and the rest of the world could go hang, at least that is what I understood. In the last year of the Civil War, as a very young man, I had fought the men from Texas at Nashville and had seen the bravery of the often shoeless young men who fought in Hood's proud Texas Brigade. Young men who had so often died with no food in their bellies, carrying empty muskets with bayonets fixed.

Having made Texas my destination, I ditched my yellow-striped blue army pants at the first town I came across in Colorado and bought a used pair of worn and faded work pants and scuffed shotgun chaps. Blending in would be my aim as post war feelings were, still even after nearly a dozen years, I was told, running strong in some places way down there.

It took a little longer than I had planned but I was not in any hurry and the chestnut, much like me, needed a long rest from time to time. Mostly I camped out and lived off the land but on occasion, in very inclement weather or needing company and a good, hot, cooked meal that did not involve finding water and cleaning pots and pans, was very necessary to my peace of mind. Couple of times I sought and was given generous hospitality at a homesteader's place or small ranch and although payment was offered, it was always turned down. Colorado seemed very much to be a state of hospitality and warmth to the weary traveller.

On one stormy night, I took shelter at an isolated and abandoned church only to find hay for the horse and a basket of cold meat pie, fruit and bread beside my bed roll when I awakened. I had not heard my visitor, and neither could I see any sign of the direction whence he or she had come, but the food warmed me and the chestnut snorted his way through the grain and hay, for all of which I left a note of thanks on paper torn from my diary, and one silver dollar.

I did not cross the Texas State line until I had travelled one-hundred or so miles through northern New Mexico then proceeded east and headed for the High Plains to the north and west of Amarillo and below the Canadian River, eventually winding up at my chosen destination, Canterville, the seat of Belton County. It was a mid-sized town, its Main Street bisected by railroad tracks virtually cutting the town in half. The lower half a collection of buildings, many of them ramshackle, several cantinas and a small mission. On the upper half, Canterville appeared to be a prosperous cattle town with several hotels, stores, a Wells Fargo bank, livery, two saloons and a white-painted church.

It was already late afternoon and my first stop was the livery stable, making sure that the chestnut was cared for after his long journey and that, should I need a mount, there were several horses of worth available. My next port of call was the bank to ensure that, should I need them in a hurry, my funds would be available. They were a wealth of information regarding the town itself. The manager, a talkative, quaintly old-fashioned, balding, wizened little figure of a man with a mouth full of crooked teeth, advised me over the top of his rimless spectacles that the Lucky Black Cat, part saloon and gambling joint and part hotel, was the best of the rest. He assured me that it would take care of most of my physical needs and was a safe place to drink, considering it was owned by George Surrette who was also the long-time county sheriff. He advised me, with a smile, not to play poker with the law, it nearly always won. I was not quite sure what the inference there was but told him I was very careful when playing games of chance.

'The cat was not so lucky for the customers then?' I asked.

'The cat wasn't lucky at all, got itself shot for crossing the path of a superstitious German peddler. Horace Watkins, the previous owner of the saloon, shot the peddler and the German killed him as he went down. Luck is not exactly a hot word around Canterville but we have very little trouble here nowadays and your money is safe in this bank, whatever your name might be.'

Good to know, I thought.

After checking the real estate office and the local newspaper office, I registered at the hotel end of the Lucky Black Cat. The desk clerk was a carbon copy of the bank manager and I guessed them to be brothers. I ordered a bath, and arranged to have my clothes laundered and a bottle of whiskey sent up to my room.

*

Late into the evening, bathed, rested and in a change of clothes, I stowed my sidearm in the chest of drawers, having noted the posted ordnance on entering the town limits, that firearms were not to be worn, before I made my way down to the saloon and ordered a beer without a head. The barkeep smiled, and I guessed it was a regular request and not one necessarily favoured by the owner who was happy to sell three quarters of a glass with a quarter of frothy air on the top. The place was busy, with only a few spaces at the bar and most of the tables taken up by suited men rather than cowhands; those I guessed drank elsewhere. Dominoes and jawing seemed to be the chosen pastimes following their evening meal.

Sheriff George Surrette was not difficult to spot. A tall figure of a man dressed in a black, town suit with a long, frock coat, a worn face and a drooping, grey moustache, topped off by a black, derby hat. He was stationed at one end of the long bar, a shot glass of whiskey in his left hand. Our eyes met in the mirror, he nodded and made his way over to fill the empty space beside me.

'Mr Luck, I believe. Word travels fast around this town. Lucky by name, lucky by nature, Mr Luck?' His voice was like walking over gravel, deep, gritty and tobacco-stained.

'Sheriff Surrette,' I said, offering him my hand. He took it and his handshake was firm but not threatening. Some men like to send a message in that simple gesture, but not so Surrette.

'Welcome to Canterville, Mr Luck. I trust your stay will be a peaceful one.'

'I hope so too, Sheriff, and most folk call me Harry or HJ.'

'And I,' he said, 'am perfectly at ease with George unless it is official business, of course.'

'And this is?' I smiled the question.

'A George day. Anything I can help you with let me know. An ex-military man I am guessing?'

'It is that obvious?'

'I was in the army before I got behind a badge. It takes one to know one. Parade-ground straight, from your bearing I would guess you to have been an officer. I watched you ride into town, no mistaking your seat.'

'I just mustered out a few weeks back. It will take a while to blend in I guess.'

'From up north?'

'Wyoming, Fort Laramie.'

'A long ride. Are you looking for work or what? Maybe I can help.'

'Actually, you may be able to help. I am looking to settle, buy a small spread in this part of the country, make it work for me. I looked in at the real estate office but it was closed as was the newspaper office.'

He laughed a belly laugh as rugged as his voice. 'Charlie Beam and Jim Hayes, two of a kind, they spend more of their time fishing than working. Tell you what, you call by the office tomorrow around noon, I will show you a couple of likely places within a leisurely ride from town, one of them only very recently on the market.'

We shook hands again and the big man silently moved back along the bar to where it turned against the wall. His place, an all-around clear view of the large bar area.

CHAPTER TWO

THE HORSESHOE BRAND

It was a fine morning, the promise of rain the evening before had not been kept and only a gentle breeze drifted along the escarpment that led to the distant wooded mountains. After a breakfast of eggs over easy and a slice of ham, I hired a bay from the livery *remuda* and walked the animal along the street to the long, white, adobe county courthouse which also held the town jail, court room and sheriff's office. The Lone Star flag whispered listlessly in the breeze from its tall, white flagpole and doves were seated along the length of the brass barrel of the vintage canon standing guard on the judiciary of Texas. The only signs of life, a large black mare tied to the hitching rail and the scarecrow frame of a grey, elderly man slumped on the courthouse steps, staring at the ground in front of him. His shoes were run-down and his suit had not seen an iron in a coon's age. His hat was a crumpled mess, the cuffs of his shirt were frayed and grubby, his grey hair lank, his face unshaven. Within a few moments Surrette emerged through the double doors, paused by the man and gave him some loose change. The man smiled a tired smile up at him but did not get to his feet. I could not hear the words that passed between them but the look of sadness, or maybe it was exasperation on Surrette's face, told me this was a regular and painful ordeal for both of them.

'Good morning, Mr Luck. I trust you slept well?'

I nodded. Calling me by my surname seemed to amuse him for some odd reason. For a big man on a tall horse he swung easily up on to the black leather concho-decorated saddle, settled there and giving a nod to the grey man, he turned his animal to the west and I followed, riding side by side down Main Street to the open country beyond Canterville's town limits.

It was autumn, golden covered in a mixture of short prairie and buffalo grass, an undulating open range as far as the eye could see. Large stands of trees, mainly cottonwood, aspen with the occasional live oak and to our left on the distant higher rocky ground, spruce, juniper, piñon pine and mesquite. The last of the summer's wildflowers gathered in the more sheltered areas, bluebonnet, daisy and paintbrush were the most prevalent. Our passage raised small clouds of insects and a cottontail or two but the only birdlife apart from the larks, were a hunting pair of high-flying red-tailed hawks and a lone raven.

After a half hour's gentle ride, we reined in our horses on a high ridge, looked down on a grassy, wooded landscape and dismounted, sharing a swig from Surrette's hip flask. He corked the flask and rolled himself a cigarette while I took out my pipe and stuffed the bowl to the brim, tamped it down and fired it with a thumb-struck blue-topped match.

Surrette was the first to break the silence. 'Can you really imagine a time when the whole plateau in front of us would have been darkened by buffalo? Can you imagine what a sight that must have been, Mr Luck?'

'Not really,' I said. 'Hard to imagine so many were killed for little more than to starve the Comanche onto reservations, much as they have done with the Sioux and the Cheyenne up to the north.'

'Hard to fathom the minds of men. I gave up on that a long time ago.'

I wondered if that were true but said nothing.

'Just a guess, Mr Luck, but is that why you quit the army?'

I did not answer right away, studying instead the glowing bowl of my pipe and the smoke drifting out from my mouth, but there was something I liked about the big man. 'I do not believe you have stopped fathoming men, Sheriff. It would be a hard habit to break.'

He gave his gravelly chuckle then carefully stubbing out his cigarette, remounted and we rode on a couple of miles in absolute silence.

I have heard about and read of people falling in love at first sight but have always believed myself to be too much of a realist to believe in such nonsense. Places, like people, need careful study before leaping in without thought or care, and a given set of circumstances has been reasoned through and dismissed when the first glow has died. But I could well have been wrong about that.

We emerged down from the low grassy ridge, through a stand of oak trees on to a small plain and crossed a clear, shallow, cold-water stream interspersed at intervals with deep fishing holes and rocky outcrops. The sandy banks were littered with deer spoors and the tracks of web-footed, wading birds. The creek would no doubt be fed constantly by the rain-swept distant hills and the snow melt in spring and summer. A hundred or so yards from the creek a windmill creaked and fed a large water tank. A little way beyond that stood a long, wide, timber-porched cabin with a stone chimney at each end; a small barn to the left of that and a good-sized pole corral in need of a little attention. Cottonwoods to the rear of the cabin set the scene almost too perfectly. I just stared at it, hypnotised by the sheer simplicity of it.

Surrette said very quietly, 'See something you like, Mr Luck?' Then that gravelly chuckle again.

I did not answer him but instead climbed down from the saddle and loosening the bay's cinch, led the animal down to the water's edge.

'You want to check out the cabin? We can, it's empty.'

'How come?' I asked.

'A foreclosure, mortgage arrears but mostly back taxes; previous owner had some bad luck, went broke. County owns it now.' He smiled again. 'I get a commission if I sell it. Good acreage but not too big, price is a steal. One word of warning though, most folk around here think it is a bad luck property. Built partly on a Comanche sacred burial site, that's why no takers. You believe in stuff like that, Mr Luck?'

'A man makes his own luck, George. That's what I believe anyway.'

'Big waves happen, son.'

'What kind of bad luck did the previous owner have?' I asked, not taking my eyes from the scene in front of me, my mind already racing ahead, back to town, the bank, my money, papers signed, a real home at last.

'Cholera, out of the blue, took his wife and two kids, all three are buried in back out by the tall oak tree. He couldn't get over it, took to drinking alone, tried to kill himself a couple of times and couldn't even do that properly. He was a friend of mine.'

'I'm sorry, I truly am, but that was then and this is now, my chance to start over and I cannot be worrying about things that might never happen, or the Comanche graves. I will respect them if I find them.'

'Good to hear it. Do you want to look inside or head back for supper? We should be there before dark.'

'If we ride hard we should be in time to catch the bank, see an attorney and seal this deal.'

'A man in a hurry?'

'You are damned right about that, Sheriff.'

The following morning, after a restless night of worrying something would go wrong, I met with George Surrette and the wizened little Wells Fargo bank manager in the dusty office of Attorney at Law Thomas Arthur Fisk and signed the deeds to the ranch. The transaction was expedited for the county by the sheriff, witnessed by his deputy Billy

Cole and a little after noon I was the owner of a reasonably sized, compact ranch currently recognized as, and carrying the registered brand of the Horseshoe. Later following a celebratory drink with Surrette, his deputy and the attorney, I organised the purchase of a buckboard, pulling horse and supplies for the winter.

The bumpy ride out to the ranch took a little longer by buckboard as there was no defined trail. I guessed there soon would be, but it would take time and I had plenty of that. For the moment though, the heavy four-wheeler would not travel the route we had taken on the saddle horses the previous day. The chestnut was content to trot behind and when loosed into the corral alongside of the pulling horse, a big footed roan, she raced around for a minute or two before rolling in the dust. I had become quite attached to the big animal and was happy that she was happy.

The interior of the cabin was much as I expected it to be, carefully and thoughtfully constructed for a young family. Two bedrooms, indoor facilities, a kitchen area with cooking range, a hand pump and sink, a comfortable-looking large lounge area with dining table and two stone fireplaces, one at each end. The larger of the two had a leather armchair each side of it seemingly almost too big to go through the cabin doorway and I wondered fancifully if the unlucky previous owner had built the house around them.

The close-boarded floor was dusty and there was a smell of dampness about the place and I guessed it had been empty for some time. I lit both fires and fed them from a stack of logs piled each side of the hearth. I also fired up the range and got some coffee on the boil while I made a list of things needed and which I had, in my haste, forgotten to buy, one of them being tobacco for my pipe.

Sitting out on the veranda on that first night was memorable. I had a bottle of whiskey to sip, my pipe, night birds calling and the occasional restless snort from the chestnut. Enjoying my new-found home, I did not for one moment think of the fate of the previous owner; time and indifference are not things to mess with.

George Surrette said, 'You seem like a very happy man, Mr Luck and I have a present for you.' He reached behind his desk and presented me with a newly-forged branding-iron fashioned in the shape of a horseshoe with a capital letter L in its centre.

I thanked him, smiled and asked, 'Are you going to call me that forever?'

'Forever is a long time but, yes, I like the sound of it and maybe it will be a good omen for you. Help to keep the phantom Comanche at bay.'

'Phantom Comanche? First I have heard of him.'

'Didn't want to spoil your day.'

I shrugged. 'You haven't. I have to drop off a list at a couple of the stores then heading for a hot meal at the Black Cat. I may stay overnight depending how late it is and on the weather. It's cold and could be wet.'

'Winter is just around the corner; hot summers and short but cold winters hereabouts, you never have time to get bored. Pick me up here when you are ready, we can have a snort of the good stuff before supper and not that forty-rod I sell behind the bar.'

He was right. Even wrapped in my long, sheepskin coat I felt the bite of the northerly wind, and the temptation of eating someone else's cooking was too much. I delivered my supplies order to the store and asked that they be filled by first thing in the morning, then drove the buckboard to the livery, giving the stable boy a quarter to unhitch the roan, feed him and stable him for the night. That done I booked into the hotel, got my hair cut and made my way down toward the courthouse. Just as I passed the closed bank, a bundle of rags stirred in the recess of the doorway and the scarecrow of the old man I had seen mooch a coin from the sheriff, emerged from out of the heap. In the glow of the flickering, kerosene street lamps, his unshaven face appeared even more pallid, the grey eyes watery and the stale stink of his clothing offensive to my nostrils. I paused, wondering what his connection to Surrette might be.

'You the fellow as bought the Horseshoe, mister?'

His voice was cracked and smoky, his breath coming in short puffs, the vapour in the chilly air rank with the stink of stale tobacco and beer.

I nodded and automatically drew some coins from my jacket pocket.

'No, mister, keep it, I don't want your money. I want your promise.' He stepped back to the shadows as if aware of his effect on me.

'Promise? I don't understand you, sir.'

'I want your promise you will tend the graves out there by the live oak back of the house.'

'What is that to you?'

I offered him the coins again but he waved them away. 'Just your promise is all.'

'OK, if it makes you happy, you have my word on that.'

He smiled. 'Thank you, mister, thank you.' He turned back to the doorway, picked up an old blanket, walked past me and vanished down the nearby alley.

I watched his departure, wondering to myself what the hell was that all about? Not having an answer, I continued my interrupted journey to the courthouse, arriving only seconds before the rain.

CHAPTER THREE

A GUNFIGHT

Surrette was seated behind his desk, a bottle of bourbon and two shot glasses at the ready. The office was cold and I huddled my jacket around me, conscious that it hid my revolver, wondering if I should leave it with him. I had forgotten about the town ordnance forbidding the carrying of weapons within the town limits.

'Something on your mind, Mr Luck?' Again, that quick smile as he filled our glasses to the brim. 'Here's to the Horseshoe and the Comanche dead.'

He downed his in a single swallow, but I sipped

at mine, studying the amber liquid in the dim light from the single office lamp.

'Something on your mind?'

'A curious thing just happened out by the bank,' I said.

'And that would be?'

I recounted my meeting with the tramp, wondering why he would not take the money he so obviously needed and why my promise meant so much to him.

Surrette gave a deep sigh, and taking out the makings rolled himself a cigarette before topping up his glass, ignoring mine. 'That would be Jack Pelham and he's not an old man. He just looks like one,' he said quietly. 'The previous owner of the Horseshoe, the man who could not kill himself. The graves are for Janine his wife, Jack junior and his daughter Jill, his two kids; eight and eleven I believe they were.'

'He cannot blame himself for their deaths. Cholera is just bad luck is all.'

'He can and he does. Thinks if he had not brought them out here, had tried harder to make a go of it in Washington where he had a small business, they would still be alive.'

'It doesn't work like that. . .' but my words were interrupted by the door crashing open and the young deputy Billy Cole falling across the threshold, his face covered in blood.

Surrette was first to reach the deputy and together we got him on to the back-room cot the sheriff used when he had to sleep over. He vanished for a moment and returned with a white basin and cloth and began wiping the blood from the boy's face. 'What the hell happened, Billy? Your Goddamned nose is broke.'

Tears were streaming down the youngster's face; that sometimes happens with a broken nose, it makes the eyes water. 'Three drifters, never seen them before, got the Black Cat treed. Just busted in, beat up on Henry and herded the rest of the customers into a corner; they went like sheep. I tried to take them on but they took my gun, kicked my ass and threw me out on to the street. Took no never mind of my badge.'

Surrette swore and said, 'Damnation! Long time since we had trouble like that. I'd best get over there before something really bad happens. You sit tight with Billy for me.'

'To hell with that,' I said, as I reached past him to the big gunrack, selected a sawed-off shotgun and some shells from the cartridge box, shook them to make certain they were fully charged before I opened the gun's breech and dropped them in. I snapped the gun closed and followed him out on to the wet sidewalk.

We moved swiftly down Main Street and as we neared the saloon I touched his arm and he paused midstride.

'Back door open?' I asked.

'Yes, always. A single door, no window. When I go in, I will step to my right.'

'That will do, give me one minute.' And with that I ducked down the dark alley that ran beside the Lucky Black Cat hotel and saloon and, just before I reached the door, I shucked my sheepskin.

I am very proficient with a sidearm and the Colt Army .44.40 with its long barrel was tooled to my specification, the walnut grips fashioned to my hand. I was not a fast draw but when it was out and in my hand, that Colt hit the mark every time without me taking deliberate aim. Speed is not everything, no point being the fastest on the pull if you can't hit the side of a barn when the gun is out. The analogy of tortoise and the hare springs to mind.

I cocked both hammers on the shotgun and opened the door and found myself looking across the long bar at the open double doors just as Surrette stepped through them and sidestepped to his right.

Billy had been correct. There were three of them, scruffy roughnecks all. One was in front of me but blocked mostly by the slumped body of Henry the bartender. Another was on the gallery above the left side of the saloon and the third was way over to Surrette's left, out of his view. Thomas Arthur Fisk, the attorney, was laying prone on the saw-dusted floor and I could not tell if he was alive or dead. All three gunmen had weapons in their hands so there was no need for formalities.

Surrette took the gunman in front of me with a single shot before taking a round from the hidden man to his left. He was a stubby fellow and I gave him both barrels, blowing him off his feet and out through the window. The broken glass was still falling as I dropped the shotgun, pulled the Colt and hammered the third man on the gallery with two chest shots. He bounced backwards against the wall and then fell forward, over the rail and landed with a thud close to where Fisk was stretched out.

It was over in seconds. Three dead, no-account, saddle tramps, drunk and looking for trouble and a wounded county sheriff, a bullet having hit him in his left thigh. Surrette would probably have a slight limp for the rest of his life but it could have been worse.

It turned out that Fisk had fainted when the stubby gunman had broken Billy's nose and kicked him out on to Main Street.

George Surrette was staring at me hard, probably to help ease the pain visited upon him by Doc McAlpine's pointed probe as he dug for the round taken in the thigh by the big lawman.

'Fancy handgun shooting for a soldier, Mr Luck.'

'I have had some practice, Sheriff.'

'You carrying that piece when you rode into town?'

'Not intentionally. I forgot about the no-carry notice.'

'That's a twenty-dollar fine then. Pay it before you leave town.'

'Are you serious?'

'Very. Either that or I could retrospectively appoint you as a part-time deputy. Which do you prefer?'

'Neither very much, but I will take the part-time badge because I'm running a little short on cash at present.'

'Good, then I will swear you in later and see you in church on Sunday, twelve o'clock sharp. That's my ruling. Now get out of my sight, you trouble me somewhat.'

There was a twinkle in his blue eyes, but I think, at least in part, he was serious. He turned his attention to the doctor. 'Damn it, Doc, isn't there a quicker way?'

'Well, I could take your leg off, take it back to my office and fish around for the slug another day.'

'Damn it all to hell.' Those were the last words I heard from him as I quietly closed the door and carrying his good bottle of bourbon in my deep, jacket pocket, made my way back to the hotel. I noted the bundle of ragged blankets back in the Wells Fargo doorway but there was no sign of Jack Pelham.

CHAPTER FOUR

WE GATHERED AT THE RIVER

Sunday was never my favourite day, not now and not back when I was a soldier. It was a nothing kind of day, especially if you were stuck in the Fort. If the weather was fair, then pitching horse-shoes passed some of the time, barracks poker for peanuts or a book from the post library. All of which had to follow the inevitable church parade and dreary, righteous sermon given by a sanctimonious padre everyone knew to be sleeping with the post commander's wife. Still, it would get me away from the ranch for a few hours and from my own company which, following the killing of two men, even if the circumstances of the killings justified such an act of violence, did not sit well with me. Surrette identified the trio as some of the last dregs of the Comancheros, part of a larger outfit that operated way over in south New Mexico Territory and further south of the line. He hoped there would be no repercussions as there was little money to be earned in revenge killings and he thought it unlikely, at least in the immediate future.

Following an early night and a restless sleep, I awoke early, lit the stove, washed, shaved, cooked some breakfast and settled on the porch, concentrating on rolling a morning cigarette and waited for the full sunrise. A splash of the last of Surrette's bourbon sweetened my morning coffee and, in my newly-purchased town suit, I felt ready to meet the day and whatever it had to offer.

It did not begin exactly as I expected. When I looked up from my finished quirly, he was there in my front yard, astride a bare-backed, piebald pony with large red, white and black roundels painted on the animal's sturdy shoulders. He was dressed head to foot in buckskin, a single eagle feather in his headband and a Henry repeating rifle across his knees. His age was difficult to determine even at the short distance across the yard. His face was brown and crinkled like old leather, with dark eyes sparkling like black diamonds set deeply under a furrowed brow, telling me he was not a young man.

I raised my hand to him but did not get to my feet.

He did not acknowledge my greeting in any way and we played the staring game. After a couple of minutes, he reined the pony's head to the right and walked the animal out of the yard, down the slight incline through the trees and within minutes was lost to my view. Was that the Comanche Surrette had alluded to, I wondered?

There were several horses twitching and fly swatting with their tails at the hitching rail in front of the white, newly-painted church as well a dozen or so rigs. I hoped I was not the last to arrive; something very daunting about walking into a church where the service has already begun, and you must walk the entire length of the aisle to the one vacant seat, usually in the front row. But that is exactly as it worked out. I hung my hat on the rack by the porch door and my head in shame as I shuffled forward under the cheerful eye of the deacon, George Surrette, who paused in his morning delivery to introduce me to an amused congregation.

'This, my friends, is Mr Harry Luck, the newest member of our growing community and new owner of the Horseshoe Ranch. He is also my new part-time deputy. I hope you will welcome him as I have. It is just possible that he was sent here to save my life or maybe to enrich his own. Either way, I trust he has a fine voice and will now lead us in

Shall we gather at the River. Bonnie, my dear, will you give, Mr Luck a note please?'

Bonnie Luxford was a dark-haired, dark-eyed, straight-backed young woman whom I guessed to be in her early thirties. She was handsome, and her smile lit up the room as she turned to me and nodded her head. I think she immediately saw my squirming discomfort and hit a note, and with the lustiest of contralto voices, burst into song. I followed, as did to my great relief, the whole congregation, caught up in the magic of the moment.

We sang some good hymns, listened to a gentle sermon on the rights and wrongs of life in general, and of loyalty in particular, and then streamed outside into the bright, morning sunshine. With my worn-out army campaign hat in my left hand, I near wore out my right hand shaking the offered hands of just about the whole congregation, and when that ordeal was over, moved into the shade beneath a cottonwood tree, pulled the makings from my jacket pocket and rolled a cigarette, noting that my hands were trembling slightly. I am no performer.

'That was rather cruel of George to face you with that particular task, Mr Luck. I hope you know that I had no part of it. He had even reserved that pew for you.' It was Bonnie Luxford. 'He must like you a great deal to go to so much trouble, but how did he know you would be late, I wonder?'

I shook her offered hand and held it a moment longer than was necessary. 'That's easy. He told me the service started at noon and not eleven forty-five, and he failed to tell me he was the deacon as well as the county sheriff.'

'I do believe he sees them as one and the same job.'

We both laughed.

'Want to share your amusement with me?' George Surrette joined us. He was limping and leaning heavily on a dark, cherrywood cane. He had a broad smile on his weathered face, half concealed by the big moustache but still clearly visible.

'I was just telling Mr Luck that it was mean of you not to tell him you were the deacon and that you planned the whole thing.'

'No meanness intended, my dear.'

'I hope not,' she said, smiling at him, enjoying the exchange. 'I will see you in a moment or two, Mr Luck. Now I have refreshment duties to attend to.' And then she was gone.

Surrette turned his attention back to me again. 'Lovely woman. She means a great deal to me.'

I thought I detected the merest hint of a warning in his soft voice.

I nodded and said, 'Yes, delightful.'

'You know your hymns, Mr Luck, and you have a sturdy voice, but are you really a God-fearing man I wonder?'

'I would not worship a God I was afraid of, Sheriff, and that's a fact.'

'A fact it may be, but not really an answer, is it?'

'I have attended hundreds of church parades, sung a lot of hymns and said an equal number of prayers over the dead I have buried and sometimes killed. I have buried men in rough graves on the battlefield and later dug them up and reburied them in consecrated ground, but I have never yet come to terms with the broad, catch-all religion so often preached. That answer your question?'

'Not really, but we can talk about it more at some other time. Right now we join the congregation in the back yard for some lemonade and homemade apple pie.' He patted the shape of his hip flask concealed in the fold of his frock coat. 'The lemonade will be suitably enhanced, of course.'

Most of the rest of the early afternoon I spent talking to folk, generally mixing and taking what sounded like good advice from the local ranchers in the congregation. Their ladies mostly bemoaned the oncoming winter which was, even in the bright sunshine, adding an early-evening bite to the air. I did not get another opportunity to speak with Bonnie Luxford, who seemed to be everywhere and everything to everyone. I found Surrette seated on the bench that folded itself neatly around a live oak, and carrying my lemonade in one hand, a plate of apple pie in the other, I joined him there. He indicated my glass and I held it out for a large splash of amber liquid which I hoped was his best bourbon. It was.

'Take the weight off for a while, Mr Luck,' he said.

I sat down, stretched my legs out in front of me, sipped the lemonade and nibbled on my pie. 'Why didn't you mention you were a pastor here?' I asked.

'Didn't seem relevant is all.'

'You the mayor as well, by any chance?'

He laughed. 'Not sure I am allowed by law to hold both offices at once and the same time but it is a thought and I will check on that. Tubby Harlan, our current mayor, could do with getting a run for his money. Are you interested in politics? Could be an opening for you there.'

'Not in any way,' I said, adding, 'I had a visitor this morning.'

'Oh, and that would be?'

'An old, a very old Comanche on a painted horse. He the one you mentioned?'

'Must be. Only one around here now, last of them I guess. Most of them are either dead or on the reservation in Oklahoma. Lives in a cave somewhere up on the Horseshoe. Did you ask him what he wanted?'

'No, he wasn't very talkative, carried a Henry rifle.'

'Some gun, that. Pity about the calibre though.'

'Do you have any idea as to what he might have wanted of me?'

'Just checking you out, I guess. He answers, if he answers at all, to the name of Wolf. I use him sometimes if we need a tracker. He's a damned good one. Some say he is the keeper of the Comanch' graveyard up a little beyond where Jack Pelham's family are buried and not too far from the summer cabin he was building for them before the cholera struck.'

'I found the cabin. Done some work on it myself, roof leaked, been getting it ready and dry for the winter. I did not see any sign of graves around there other than those of the Pelhams.'

'Look again, look harder about a mile higher than the cabin. They say there were seventeen of them, women and children mostly, killed by the black federal soldiers under Colonel Mackenzie's command. I don't know if that holds true, but they are there, and I do believe he watches over the graves to see they are not desecrated as other Indian graves have been for skulls, bones, artefacts and the like. They are the savages and we are the civilized people, eh?' He paused. 'Who would have believed it possible.'

It wasn't a question.

As the last of the congregation dispersed into the fading light, a buggy turned up for Surrette, driven by his full-time deputy Billy Cole, the boy sporting two black eyes and a swollen nose. As Surrette climbed awkwardly on to the swaying rig he turned to me. 'That's Bonnie's rig by the tree. Will you see to it she gets home safely for me? Official duty of course, not pleasure. Fifty cents an hour so don't take too long about it.'

Was he smiling under that moustache? I could not be sure, but I said that I would see to it and waved him off.

I found her on the back porch of the church and was disappointed to see that she was not alone but in the company of a matronly woman of considerable girth, which kind of ruled out my hope of tying off the chestnut behind the rig and riding a moonlit night ride in the buggy alongside her. She turned as I approached, and smiled that same charming smile she had given me in the church. Practised?

'My Aunt Matilda. Aunty, this is Mr Luck.' The woman nodded.

'The sheriff asked me to escort you ladies home. Official business earns me four bits an hour so don't hurry,' I said, taking off my hat.

'Indeed, we will hurry, sir, it is going to be a cold night. Winter is knocking on the door.'

'Yes, I have been told that,' I said, 'many times.'

I helped them with their baskets and hampers, made sure they had blankets over their knees, and stood back as Bonnie Luxford took up the reins and trotted the pulling horse forward. I rode off to the right, wondering if my presence there was really necessary or another of George Surrette's little jokes.

Vine Street, where she had told me she lived in a rented house, was in a quiet area on the western side of the town, well away from the railroad track and the town's self-imposed dividing line. It took a little over five minutes before we were at her brick and timber cottage with a sweet-scented garden and white picket fence. I helped both ladies from the rig, holding Bonnie's waist a lot longer than I did that of her matronly aunt who hustled and bustled her niece to the front door. I said I would deliver the buggy back to the livery and bade her a quiet goodnight. I was half-way back to the gate when Bonnie reached me and touched my arm as I turned.

'I am sorry we did not have time for a conversation of any kind, Mr Luck, but if you are going to be in town tomorrow evening, perhaps we could have dinner together.'

'I would like that very much,' I said, 'and please call me Harry.'

'Here then, shall we say seven of the clock or is

that too late for you?'

'That is a quaint turn of phrase and seven of the clock is fine.'

'My daddy was a whaler out of Boston. I picked such language up from him. I miss him and Boston very much.'

'Thank you, that time suits me very well. I will be going back to the ranch first thing in the morning and be back later in the afternoon and staying over for a business meeting.'

That was a lie, but I didn't want her to think I came cheap.

CHAPTER FIVE

THE COMANCHE

I left Canterville very early the following morning after confirming my reservation for the room again that night and arrived home just as dawn was breaking. Home, that word sounded good in my mind. The first real home, other than the military, I have ever had. I turned the chestnut loose and cooked myself a big breakfast before packing some tools in my saddle bags and heading north on the roan for the cabin that Jack Pelham had been working on. It took around ten or so minutes and was mostly uphill, flattening out on a pine-wooded plateau lush with pasture, small birds and insects. There were whitetail deer tracks around the small, mountain-fed spring and it was easy to see why Pelham had chosen such an idyllic setting for a little home away from home for his family.

By a little after noon, I had finished the temporary repairs to the flat-boarded roof and replaced some of the turf used to seal it. I washed up at the stream and put some wildflowers on the graves of the mother and children. Then, remembering what Surrette had told me, I sought for and found the Comanche graves. The circle was ringed with large stones higher than the seventeen small mounds covering the bodies of the murdered Comanche women and children. I picked more wildflowers, mostly bluebonnets, probably the last of the summer's crop, and sprinkled them over and around the graves. Strange how a bunch of pretty, sweet-smelling flowers can beautify the site of such a bloody and senseless slaughter. Satisfied with my efforts, I settled my backside on a warm rock and rolled myself a cigarette and, as I fired it, I saw through the smoke, the silent, grey-haired Comanche standing at the edge of the clearing, his Henry at the trail in one hand and the reins of his pony in the other. I drew gently on the quirly and waited.

Nothing.

Finally, I pointed to the Bull Durham sack of tobacco on the stone beside me and nodded. He moved toward me through the short grass, dropped the pony's reins and set the rifle against the rock upon which I was sitting and within easy reach of my hand. I took it to be a gesture of trust, and smiled. He did not return the smile but reached for the tobacco and rolled a thick log of a quirly, lighting it and slowly exhaling a cloud of smoke. He waved his hand in the direction of the burial ground and nodded approvingly. Halfway through the cigarette he got to his feet, crushed the smoking end between thumb and forefinger and put the remainder in his pocket. He stripped off a couple of Rizla papers from the sack and added them to his haul then, without a word, picked up the Henry and leading the pony, walked out of the clearing.

I frittered away the rest of the day doing small, odd jobs around the ranch house with one eye on the weather and the other on my pocket-watch. Leaving at mid-afternoon, I was back at the hotel in time for a bath, a shave and a change of clothes. I bought what Henry, the Black Cat bartender, assured was a good bottle of red wine and at exactly ten minutes to seven, I nervously headed out on the short walk to the house of Bonnie Luxford. It was a promising, bright, moonlit night and I hoped that fortune would favour the brave.

She answered the door only seconds after I had tapped the iron knocker, laughing. 'I saw you walking up the street. You looked as if you might be going to a funeral. Why so glum, sir?'

'Harry,' I said, 'remember me?'

She laughed again and examined the label on the bottle and thanked me with the usual, you really shouldn't have bothered remark so common in such situations adding, 'Let me take your coat and hat.' She examined the latter at some length. 'Been with you for a while I imagine?'

'Nearly ten years to the day and I would not change it for the world.' I took off my jacket and immediately noted her look of disapproval at the sight of my black, tooled-leather gunbelt and holstered Colt revolver. I undid the buckle and hung the rig beside my jacket.

'Isn't it against the law to carry such a weapon in Canterville?' she asked.

'Not if you are a sheriff's deputy,' I said, sensing the merest hint of irritation in her words. 'I'm told it goes with the badge, on or off duty.'

She gave a brief smile followed by a sniff and turned back toward the large dining room. There was a fire burning in the grate, the room was warm, and the table set for two, but I felt I had somehow made a bad start and was not too sure how to put it right. Perhaps my concern was unfounded, because when she returned from the kitchen carrying a large tray of gravy-covered roast chicken and a platter of vegetables, her bright smile was back in place.

The evening, like the wine, vanished quickly. She played the piano and sang Lorena for me at my request and I joined in the chorus, having a fair but not overpowering country voice. She laughed a lot at my effort but not cruelly, raising her hand for the higher notes and lowering when it got too high.

The clock on the mantle shelf chimed ten o'clock and she jumped. 'My goodness, so late. Aunty will be back shortly now.'

'I had best be on my way then. I don't want to ruin your reputation.'

'No fear of that, Harry. I am the virgin angel of Canterville, worshipped by all thanks to George Surrette, your new boss.'

'Part-time boss that is,' I said.

'Whatever. I want to apologise for my manner when you came in, it was the sight of your firearm. I cannot abide violence in any form. It was strange enough for me to be wining and dining here in my lounge with a man who only a few days ago shot and killed two men not five-hundred yards from here. That, without having his weapon of choice hanging on my hat rack, was a little unsettling.'

The wine had deepened her voice, her words came more slowly than before. 'It's the West,' I said, as if that meant anything to her. 'It is still a new land, raw and unsettled in many parts. It abounds with greed; men grow rich out here and money attracts violence. It is a land of choice, one side of the law or the other and, fortunately, most choose the right side.'

'And you, Harry Luck, have you chosen the right side? So right that you feel the need to carry a gun when visiting a friend for supper.'

It wasn't a discussion I wanted to get into and I was struggling for a response when the front door opened, and her aunt bustled through the room, complaining about the cold, ignoring me and warming her bulky backside in front of the fire, and all three things in a matter of seconds.

I was alone, and yet the hotel room felt crowded with me, the two dead Comancheros, the old Comanche and the young rebel I had killed in Nashville at the dying end of the Civil War. The soldier had stepped out from the dark-grey smoke in front of me, heedless of the cannons behind him. He must have charged unseen in the confusion of battle, hidden by the smoke and straight through the ranks of the artillery men. He stood there, seemingly as surprised to see me as I was to see him. He was a ragged scarecrow of a young soldier. His grey uniform was in tatters, a battered kepi on his head held firm by its chinstrap. He had no shoes and very little left of his filthy socks. He was of my age, maybe even a tad younger; it was difficult to tell. He carried a musket with bayonet fixed and charged at me, yelling at the top of his voice. It took three rounds from my Remington pistol to stop him, even so his charge carried him to within three feet of me and he drove the spike into the soft ground between my feet and fell forward, propped up by the stock of the empty musket. He stared at me long and hard. I had never believed such hatred in a human face possible. He tried to speak but his mouth was filled with blood and his head very slowly slumped forward. His eyes were still wide open, that hatred generated by I knew not what. What amount of hate can persuade a young man to give up his life in that way?

I did not know the answer that day and do not know it now but something in that moment of my life struck a chord with Bonnie Luxford's words. After a long while, I fell into a troubled, wine-induced sleep, still trying to recall exactly what she had said. Was it her phrase 'weapon of choice' that rankled me so? Of what choice? Another question to answer.

Putting such thoughts behind me I slept and was glad when morning came. After two coffees and a solid breakfast inside of me, I made my way back to the Horseshoe, leaving Canterville just after first light. I did not linger long at the ranch house but quickly made my way up to the cabin. I had had an idea or two on how the interior could be improved with an indoor privy, and the exterior extended a little, incorporating a lean-to for a hay store and a couple of horses with maybe a small pole corral built on to that. The day was fair although a chilly wind had settled in from the east and promised more severe weather to come. At midday, I brewed a pot of coffee on an improvised ring-stoned fire pit a little way from the cabin and paused for a short rest.

The Comanche came out of the woods, moving quietly and leading his pony. He settled beside me, rested his rifle against his knee, picked up my tobacco and rolled another fat one. I fetched a second cup from the cabin and poured him a coffee from the blackened pot. He sipped the coffee but did not light the quirly, instead looked over the rim of his cup and asked, 'Are you expecting a visitor?' It was the first time I had heard his voice. The words were softly spoken, little above a whisper like the sound of a gentle wind through the long grass of the distant plains, not at all as I had imagined it would be. It was not the voice of an old Comanche, no tribal speech inflection, almost straight out of West Point.

'No,' I said, 'I am not.'

'Well, you have one now.'

I swept the distant meadow and tree-line but could see no sign of a rider.

He stared down at his feet. 'It's a woman visitor.'

'I don't believe so,' I said.

'Well, believe it,' he said.

Getting to my feet, I asked, 'Do you know her

name?' My words were laced with a heavy hint of sarcasm that I supposed to be lost on him.

'Give me a minute on that one,' he said, with an equal hint of sarcasm.

I walked to the edge of the clearing and watched with both delight and surprise as Bonnie Luxford broke through the tree-line. She was riding a lovely, long-maned, buckskin mare. Her wide-brimmed straw hat sat firmly on her head, held there by a colourful ribbon. She sat the big, concho-decorated saddle I recognized as Surrette's, with a gentle ease. Her long legs encased in a divided, tan leather skirt, a quilted jacket wrapped around her and a plain, black bandana at her throat. She reined the horse to a stop in front of me. 'Are you accepting visitors, today, Mr Harry Luck?'

I reached out and took the horse's bridle and held it while she sprang lightly from the saddle. 'Always, but two in one day is a bit unusual.'

'Two?' She looked over my shoulder.

I turned around, but the old Comanche was not there, and neither was his pony, my makings or the coffee cup. I turned back to her. She gave me a questioning look and I responded rather lamely with, 'There was a black bear here a moment or two ago.'

'A bear, this low down the mountain?'

'Lovely to see you,' I said, changing the subject.

'Would you like a coffee? There's a fresh pot on the brew but we will have to share. I seem to be short of mugs.'

'I would love one, straight out of the pot if needs be.'

The coffee was still hot and she nursed the cup with both hands, warming them.

'This is an unexpected visit, but it is sure enough lovely to see you.'

'I hope you do not mind. I felt I needed to talk with you more, longer. I feel I may have given you the wrong impression of my thinking of you. It was not my intention to be rude or unkind.'

'I never thought for a moment it was,' I said.

'George tells me you are an honourable man, seems he has been doing some checking on you. I hope you do not mind that he has?'

'I expected him to do just that. He is not the sort of man to hand over a county badge without knowing anything about the man walking behind it. He lend you that saddle?'

'And the horse. Her name is Mary, pride of his *remuda*. He owns a small horse ranch several miles to the west of Canterville.'

County sheriff, pastor, bar and hotel owner, horse rancher? I wondered what other pies George Surrette had his fingers in.

'Busy man is George,' I said.

'Yes, indeed he is,' she replied, a hint of laughter

in her voice. 'Is your stove fired up? I have apple pie.'

'It darned soon will be,' I said, holding the mare's head as she remounted, and after killing the fire, we made our way side by side down to the main building.

The apple pie was crusty and a delight to eat and I supplied a bottle of wine, again purchased from Henry at the Lucky Black Cat. We ate and drank and bantered but I had a feeling her visit was not simply to be entertained.

Washing the dishes, I broke the mood, giving her a way in to whatever it was she wanted to say. 'Exactly what did George Surrette discover that you could not have done by simply asking me outright?'

'Oh, I guess I could have, eventually, but I am aiming to return to Boston shortly and did not want to leave without talking to you.'

'That is a hell of a shame. Folk like you are needed out here.'

'Not really. This wild country needs men like you and George, armed men who make the place safe by walking the streets on dark nights while the rest of us sleep. Not too much need for that in Boston, I am happy to say. Do you miss the army life, Harry?'

'My comrades, yes, but the army, no. It is a suppressive force, not the benign protective service it should be. Much, if not all, is directed by a few grey suits in Washington who have never been west of the Mississippi River. They have no idea just what it is they are destroying.'

'You were a soldier for many years. Once you were nearly cashiered for assaulting a fellow officer but your dedication to the service was recognized and the charges were dropped.' She smiled and continued as if reading from an army charge sheet.

'You were involved in Indian affairs and objected to Sherman's tactics of a war of attrition against the tribes of the northern plains, and because of that you resigned your commission. It is on record that you were offered a job as chief scout but refused for the same reason. Your last commanding officer was reluctant to accept your resignation, but you quit anyway. It is George's submission that you are a good man, and that, by any measure is some recommendation.'

'You remember all of that?' I said, with a smile. 'Did you also get my hat size?'

'As a matter of fact, I did; seven and a quarter. I was going to buy you a new one by way of an apology, but George said he doubted you would part with the one you have.'

The lightened mood was contagious, and I joined her in her laughter. 'Very astute man that George Surrette,' I said. 'But you do not owe me an apology. I understand how you feel but I was brought up to the sound of gunfire and I can see and easily distinguish between the good and the bad, and one day, sometime soon, this will be a great country and I will be proud of being part of it. Are you really set on going back to Boston, Bonnie?'

'There is nothing for me here to stay for really, Harry.'

She gazed out of the window at the lovely, lush grassof the plain below the cabin. There was a wistful tone to her deep voice and on impulse I reached out and touched her arm. 'There maybe, could be, if you wanted it,' I said quietly.

She looked at me long and hard and I sensed her confusion as she reached out and covered my hand with hers.

'I had best be getting back,' she said. 'It will be dark soon.'

I rode beside her in silence right to her white-painted gate, tipped my hat, shook her hand and wished her goodnight. Then, leading the horses I walked back along Main Street to the livery stable and up to my lonely hotel room, suddenly hating the night and the darkness that had intruded upon our day.

CHAPTER SIX

A CALL TO ARMS

The week dragged slowly by. I could not think of a reasonable excuse to ride into Canterville and only had Wolf for occasional company. He came and went like the clouds that gathered over the territory, threatened to stay and vanished as quickly as they had arrived. The weather of the High Plains, as always, was very unpredictable. I had put off buying any stock until the early springtime just as I had been advised by wiser heads than mine at the Sunday church gathering. Wolf rarely entered the main house although I had invited him to, but I suspected he had adopted the smaller cabin as a shelter when the weather made his cave an unattractive proposition. I did not mind. The stove there was sometimes warm when I visited but he kept the place tidy and the woodpile stacked, kept the damp at bay and sometimes I found small game hanging by the door.

I had to admit to myself that I was rather taken by the intimacy of the little building and day-dreamed of another visit from Bonnie Luxford, that we might share it. I am not a romantic and women have not played too big a part in my frontier life and at the fort I had carefully avoided any liaison, which more often than not spelled trouble where lonely, bored men were gathered together. I had learned that the hard way. However, I did have an unexplainable attraction to the handsome Bonnie Luxford and was reluctant to let it slide by and have her wave goodbye without first expressing myself of that fact. And there was the rub. I had no idea how to do that or even if such an advance would have been welcomed. So, I fretted and worked hard on my new home, repairing the lower pole corral and building the indoor privy, lean-to and a smaller corral up at the cabin.

I oiled my Colt and fired ten rounds at an old bucket and a tossed log at variable distances just to keep my eye in; an activity that obviously, from his expression, did not meet with the old Comanche's approval. I guessed he had seen too many 'white-eyes' on his own people to ever see a measure of the skill needed to hit a distant or moving target with such a short-barrelled weapon. He was unimpressed with my marksmanship and I could not blame him for that.

On Friday, the last day of the working week for me, I decided to ride to town, see Surrette and buy some supplies. I was down to my last bottle of wine and the bacon was running low. I had asked Wolf how a few egg-laying chickens might survive but he shook his head and told me they were too much trouble and an attraction to the roaming fox, and I would probably have to shoot them. He did not approve of my killing foxes in order to protect a few noisy chickens, promising me instead that he could get me fresh eggs anytime I wanted them. I told him OK, but did not enquire as to their source. I had just finished shaving when George Surrette rode into the yard and stepped down from the big black, both were sweating from a hard ride. There was an intense seriousness to his expression, not friendly, hot and bothered, all business.

'You got coffee on?' he asked without a formal greeting of any kind.

'Yes, just on the boil.'

'Pour me one and get your gear together. You are about to earn your dollar a day the hard way.' He looked over to where the Comanche was watering and rubbing down the big black with an old grain sack.

'He with you?'

'Seems to be, hard to tell.'

'I will need him as well. Get him on board. I'm getting a posse together, meet me in town in an hour. I got to ride down to the Circle W and see if Abner Winkelman, another part-time deputy, can cover for me in town. He's too old to ride with us and I will need someone there I can trust as we may be gone a while. Then I have to pick up Joe Prior; he's on the county payroll and single.'

'Can I ask where we are going?'

'Drago Wells, forty miles north of here just below our county line. Pack your Colt and ammo and a long gun if you have one. If not, you can pick one up at the office.' He gulped down the hot coffee and without another word, turned, nodded his thanks to Wolf, mounted the black and was gone.

I put out the fire, strapped on the Colt and slid my Winchester into the saddle boot. Surrette had not said anything about supplies but I figured he would organize anything that was needed on a long trail journey. I packed tobacco, bedroll, my own reloads of ammo, the last of the bottles and a change of clothes in the saddle-bags; chose my yellow mackinaw over the duster and set off for Canterville. Wolf had heard the exchange, thought about it and opted to ride with us, saying he would pick up his gear and meet us on the north town road, he did not particularly like Canterville.

I reached town ahead of Surrette and bumped into Bonnie Luxford coming out of the Post Office. She smiled at me which lit up my morning somewhat and asked me what I was doing in town so early in the day and hoped I would call on her before I left, which lit it up even more. I explained about Surrette's posse and hoped the sudden look of concern on her face was more for me than it was for the sheriff.

'If there is anything I can do to help, please ask.'

'Just still be here when I get back,' I said, rather foolishly I suppose.

'Better than that, Harry Luck, I will visit your little cabin while you are gone and see to it that the invisible visiting bear has not torn it apart. They are apt to do that you know, especially the invisible ones.' She was laughing at me, but it did not matter.

'I will look for you there then,' I said.

'Please be careful. I think there are things we need to talk about.' She touched my arm, turned and was gone, her yellow dress swishing around her long legs. I wanted to catch up to her, ask her what she meant, but just at that moment Surrette's big black slid to a halt, stirring up little dust clouds between us.

We gathered in the sheriff's office; it was a little crowded, the air thick with tobacco smoke and perspiration. I had met Abner Winkelman and Joe

Prior at the church gathering. Winkelman had been free with his advice to me and as a long-time rancher in the area, most of it made sense. He was elderly and a little frail but obviously Surrette trusted him enough to leave him in charge of the town along with Henry Cole, Billy's older brother, Lucky Black Cat bartender and wine specialist. The other part-time deputy was Joe Prior, a thin, taciturn man. A Civil War veteran, burned brown by the sun, he could have been anywhere between fifty and a hundred years of age. I remembered him in a rumpled, grey suit pouring out the lemonade and spicing it for a selected few with his own homegrown moonshine.

Surrette banged the table and the buzz of conversation dwindled, and finally ceased. 'We all know each other here and you met Harry Luck at the church on Sunday; he is a recent addition to the county staff. I won't hold it against any man here who chooses not to ride on this posse, but I remind you it is what you are paid to do, not just ride Sunday ponies in the town rodeo-day parade. Abner and Henry will take care of things here in Canterville while we are gone.'

'Get to it, George, we all know that.' A rare word from Prior.

'OK, Jim, I will get right to it. A wild bunch hit Drago Wells last night. a dozen of them, killed my county deputy there, robbed the bank and tried to burn down the town. The fire didn't take, and the telegraph office was still functional. They wired here this morning. No doubt in my mind that they were Comancheros. Maybe part of a bigger band. Not too many of them left in this part of the country and I would guess they will hang around in the Badlands north of here and get drunk before heading southwest and back to the border or New Mexico Territory, which is very likely where they came from.'

'They will be long gone from Drago Wells by now though,' Billy Cole offered, still talking through his broken nose, although the swelling and darkness around his eyes had subsided.

'They sure enough will have, Billy, but it is my hope we can cut them off as they head south. We may have to cross the border, but I doubt the authorities there will object to that; they are as much of a threat to the Territory as they are to Texas,' Surrette said, then turning to me, asked, 'You have any thoughts on this, soldier? You have heard of the Comancheros up north, I take it?'

'Everyone has,' I said. 'Bunch of killers who used to trade with the Comanche, swapped slaves, murdered and raped their way across this part of the country. I thought they were mostly gone, along with the buffalo and the Comanche.'

'They have mostly, but where can a Comanchero go? Nowhere is the answer. They simply broke up, forming smaller groups, and raided down south of the line; unusual for them to venture this far north, but I guess they go where the money is.'

I thought about it for a long moment and then offered, 'They will surely head south, but to be sure to cut them off, we need to ride southwest, far west, and forget about the border; just go. Wolf can find us a trail through the hills and we can ambush them there. No point in trying to chase them or in hunting their trail from Drago Wells.'

'Is the Comanche coming?' Surrette asked, surprised.

'I think he likes me. We can pick him up on the north road out of town and head southwest from there. You have supplies?'

Surrette looked at Billy Cole and asked, 'All done, Billy?'

'Everything on your list, chief, and packed in gunny sacks so we don't need a pack horse to slow us down.'

'Good man. Help yourselves to ammo, boys, and let's ride. Pack some Henry shells for Wolf; he only ever seems to have a pocketful as I recall. And you, Mr Luck, put on your damned badge, pin it just over your heart, give them something to shoot at.' He smiled, and I would bet it was his first smile of the day.

CHAPTER SEVEN

THE PURSUIT

That evening, and a little saddle-sore, we camped in a dry wash twenty or so miles to the southwest of Canterville and only a dozen miles from the border with New Mexico. It was unknown country to me, rocky, sprinkled with juniper and piñyon but short on grass. We had seen ravens and red-tailed hawks but precious little else by way of wildlife. Wolf got a fire going and we had coffee laced with a little alcohol from Surrette's flask and contented ourselves with corn dodgers and beef jerky. The fire was warming and crackled cheerfully with the dry mesquite and pine cones gathered from around the campsite, giving off a homely, pleasant smell. The old Comanche, the young Billy Cole and the ageless Joe Prior were soon asleep, but I was restless and Surrette seemed to need to talk.

I moved my bedroll closer to the fire, lit my pipe from a glowing twig and waited.

'You ever hunted men before as a soldier boy?' asked.

'Only in the line of duty. Not something I really cotton to. Some would volunteer to hunt down renegades or deserters, even the occasional felon at the behest of the federal authority in the Laramie area. Lawmen were thin on the ground at the end of the Civil War.'

'They still are in some places. Out here we have the Texas Rangers of course, but they are stretched a mite thin in this part of the state. I notified them by telegraph of our intention as to what we are about here; it stretches the jurisdictional responsibilities of a county sheriff.'

'To be honest, Sheriff, I am not too sure what exactly it is that we are doing here. Me, I am just earning my dollar a day as ordered but I am not certain as to how I am expected to earn it.'

'We are on the very edge of my jurisdiction about now and tomorrow we will be crossing the Texas and county lines into New Mexico Territory. I have no jurisdiction there, but the badge will carry some weight, give us little roping room. The man in charge over there is not a major fan of the Lone Star State but neither is he too enamoured by the continued raiding of the Comancheros and using his bailiwick as a bolt hole. We will be OK just so long as we do not step too far out of line.'

'Just how far is too far?' I asked.

'Someone will surely make us aware of that when it happens.'

'Good to know,' I said, tapping out my pipe, pulling my blanket up around my chin and my hat down over my eyes. 'Good night, George,' I said.

'Good night, Mr Luck,' he replied.

We had a hot breakfast of bacon and beans to make up for our cold supper and were saddled and ready to ride just as the pale, wintery sun popped its head over the eastern horizon. Billy Cole creaked and groaned his way up onto the cold saddle of his frisky roan, but we four were hardened horsemen and quickly got our animals under control and out of the clearing, leaving him cursing the dumb animal's parentage.

Our combined thinking had been correct, and Wolf confirmed that a dozen or more riders had crossed the border with New Mexico Territory a little to the south of Drago Wells within the past twenty-four hours and we made the assumption that this bunch was likely to be our quarry. Assuming they would not be in too much of a hurry once across the line, we turned south with the intention of riding hard and getting ahead of them in time to choose a suitable site for an ambush. Hit them hard before they figured out just who it was hitting them. 'We'll confuse the hell out of the sonsofbitches,' were Surrette's exact words and so we rode hard to the south. As Surrette had explained at breakfast, this was no cotton-glove job, no quarter to be given. They had murdered a county deputy and would do the same to any one of us, given half of a chance.

Wolf knew the territory well, probably having traded with the Comancheros in his younger days when it was pretty much an all-out war with the army, and the settlers moving west to steal the land from under them. I assumed him to be a pragmatist, and having lost all hope of the buffalo coming back and a return to the old way of life, he was set to make the best of a bad job. Around midday he left us, pointing to a cone-shaped rock several miles to the west of our position, telling us there was a cold-water stream at its base just beneath a large sheltering bluff. We would need that bluff, he said, as it was going to rain hard before nightfall and that he would find us there.The heavy rain dropped out of the sky and onto us like a grey blanket just as Wolf had predicted, and we were thankful of the craggy overhang that protected us from the northerly wind that drove it. Our saddles and bedding were in the dry and the horses hobbled close by. The fire hissed now and again as the wind blustered, seemingly unable to make up its mind which direction it needed to blow in order to make our night as uncomfortable as possible.

Prior rustled up some beans and brewed some hot coffee which warmed us somewhat.

Wolf arrived a little after midnight, shook off his black slicker and gratefully took the mug of hot coffee Billy Cole poured for him while Prior led his piebald pony to shelter with the others.

I rolled the Indian a thick cigarette, lit it and passed it to him. He nodded his thanks, his hands were stone cold, and I threw his blanket around his old shoulders. 'Beans?' I asked.

'I'd rather have a steak?'

'Beans and bread is all we have.'

'That will do then.'

I ladled a generous helping on to a tin plate and dumped a slice of sourdough bread on top of it. He cleared it in a couple of minutes, belched and relit the quirly before turning to Surrette who waited patiently just beyond the glow of the fire. I guessed he knew better than to hurry the old man.

Wolf settled himself by the fire and drew deeply on the smoke I had made him. 'They are camped about four miles to the west of here. They seem to be confident there is no pursuit but did send a rider to check their backtrail. I waited his return before leaving. They appeared to be happy with his report.'

I wondered where the Comanche had learned to speak English so well; he spoke it with only the hint of an accent I could not place. Compared to the scouts of Fort Laramie and others I had encountered during my years of army service, his diction was remarkable.

'How many in the band?' Surrette asked calmly, and I suspected this routine with the old man was a familiar one to him.

'More than we expected. I counted fifteen men, fifteen saddle horses and three laden pack-horses.They must have done well in Drago Wells.'

'Comancheros?'

'Most surely, mostly Mexicans and Yaqui with a sprinkling of your people.'

'Americans?'

'No, sir, no Comanches there.'

I wondered if the subtleness of the reply was lost on Surrette but assumed it was not. 'Do you know in which direction they are headed?' asked.

'I scouted ahead of them and there is only one suitable route for their pack horses and that is through a narrow pass to the southwest of here and, were I a Comanchero and scouting for them, that is the one I would recommend, but I am not and that was in the old times before you came.' He spat in the fire and smiled. 'If we leave a little before daybreak we can ambush them there.'

'Excellent work, Wolf, now get yourself some rest,' Surrette said.

CHAPTER EIGHT

ALL SHOT TO HELL

It all seemed far too easy, but I went along with it. It wasn't really a military operation and I had no relevant knowledge of the enemy or of the terrain. Surrette seemed to know what he was about, and I took up my place on the low ridge, wondering what I would do when the shooting began. Killing from ambush was not my style and I wasn't exactly sure that I could pull down on a man without giving him fair warning of my intent. Nevertheless, I settled behind the shelter of a large rock, levered a shell into the breech of the Winchester, pushed another round into the loading port to replace it and waited for the signal, figuring to make up my mind at the last moment in the hope that the quarry would shoot first.

Surrette and Prior were lowest and nearest to the narrow defile down which Wolf had said the men would have to travel quite slowly because of their laden pack horses. He stationed himself between myself and Billy Cole on the slightly higher ground. It was perfect and hard to see where it could go wrong, but it did and quite suddenly.

There was no way to know exactly what happened, even though it happened right in front of me. One minute the leading Comanchero was moving along slowly and the next, he slid over his saddle, putting the animal between him and us, firing upwards across the leather, his first bullet striking Billy Cole sending him reeling backwards and scrabbling behind the shelter of a large boulder. The man had seen or heard something, or maybe years on the run dodging soldiers, Texas Rangers and even the Comanche, had bred within him that one element that kept him alive; the total awareness of the white-tailed buck or the wary coyote, whatever it was, it did not save his life as Surrette shot the horse from under him and then killed the falling outlaw.

And I had my answer, as lead whined and screamed off my rock, I shouldered the carbine and let fly, dropping the nearest rider to me and drawing a bead on the second. It was no longer fish in a barrel and a wall of lead rose from the canyon floor, catching Joe Prior as he moved to a more substantial place of safety, rolling him over and down the incline.

Then the lower crack of the Henry as Wolf fired and racked, fired and racked seeming to empty the magazine in a matter of seconds, clearing saddles and bowling over running men and horses. With that Henry rifle, mine and Surrette's Winchesters, it must have seemed to the killers that there was an army above their heads and they cut and ran, leaving the pack animals and their dead and wounded behind.

Seven of them made the ridge as far as I could tell through the haze of powder smoke that clung above the grey rocks. Wolf thought it to be six riders, who raced their ponies up the gradient, firing as they crashed and rattled by, turning west at the top of the divide and heading hell for leather across the short-grassed prairie. Within seconds they were out of effective range of our guns and we held back on any thought of pursuit.

Billy Cole had taken a bullet in his left shoulder and the round was quite visible, just beneath the flesh; it must have been a ricochet. Prior's wound was bad. He had a round in the hip and another in his side and was, thankfully, unconscious from a crack on the head as he fell. Surrette was cursing his luck. He had taken a ball in the thigh. 'Second time this month. Must be a damned target, hurts like hell but I can ride and so can Billy. We'll fix Joe the best we can and tie him to the saddle. He's one tough old bird.'

'Where to?' I asked, picking the little rolls of wool from my ears poked there as a protection from the concussion of the gunfire. It was efficient but they were still ringing bells in my head. 'I did not see in which direction they fled.'

'Forget them, we can get back to Canterville from here; only twenty miles or so, this canyon is on our side of the Texas line.'

Wolf slid down from his observation post on the high ground and joined us. 'They headed due west in the direction of Canterville. Looked they might go by the Horseshoe.'

My blood ran cold and I shivered.

'What's the problem, Mr Luck? Not much for them there other than maybe a few supplies. My guess is they will head for Canterville, steal what they can and head south for the Mex border.'

'Bonnie said she would visit the cabin while I was away. She could be there right now,' I said.

He stared at me long and hard. 'Then ride hard. We will catch up with you – take my black, he's faster than the chestnut. Ride damn it, ride like the wind.'

And then I was running for the big black with Wolf lumbering along at my heels. I hit the stirrup hard with my left boot and mounted on the fly.

*

If twenty years in the US Cavalry had taught me anything, it was how to ride, and Wolf was a Comanche, born to the horse. We covered the ground rapidy, the black was a magnificent ride and soon we had left the old man behind; his paint was, like its rider, built for stamina not for speed.

An hour later, I reined the big animal in on the ridge beyond the small cabin. He was lathered white with sweat and it pained me to have pushed the animal so hard, but he had one more chore to do before he rested. There was smoke coming from below, lingering in the still air above the trees; and it was not coming from the steel chimney I had installed for the small, kitchen range. Men were milling about in the yard, maybe half a dozen of them, it was hard to tell. The high-pitched scream came from the cabin and it was like a bugle call. My Colt was fully loaded as I had not used it at the canyon. Gripping the reins in my left hand, I heeled the black forward at a gallop and we charged the yard.

Firing from the saddle of a moving horse is my speciality and I dropped two of the looters even before the black had slithered to a standstill. The remaining three spurred their animals from the yard and a fourth ran from the burning cabin. I shot him in the head as he mounted a moving pony. The round went in one cheek and out of the other, spraying broken teeth and bone along with it. He fired one wild round as he galloped from the yard, but I did not return his fire, my only interest at that moment was the burning interior of the cabin.

Bonnie Luxford was prone on the floor, her yellow dress bloody, her dark eyes rolling in fear. I grabbed her up in my arms just as well-alight timber from the roof fell upon me. My shirt and right pants leg were on fire as I struggled clear and out into the open where a breathless Wolf threw the paint's blanket over me to smother the flames of my burning clothes.

I cradled her head in my arms, my eyes filled with tears, either from seeing her, the wood smoke or from the terrible pain in my back. I knew not. I just held her and heard her whispered words. 'You came, I knew you would. Oh, thank God, Harry Luck, you came.'

And that was the last time I heard her voice or any voice that day or for many days thereafter. A great darkness slowly overcame me. There was no bright light to guide me home, just the big, empty darkness that signals the end of a long journey for us all. I embraced it, welcomed it, for with it came relief from the terrible agony of my burnt body, but I was very much afraid.

The voice that reached out to me was familiar, gruff, gravelly and a little disgruntled. 'Is he ever going to wake? The lazy bastard.' That was George Surrette.

'When he's good and ready. It will hurt so he may not stay too long but it will get longer and longer each time.' That was Doc McAlpine. But who the hell were they talking about? It couldn't have been me. I was warm and comfortable and not at all hurting. I thought that maybe I should tell them that, get to my feet and them to hush. I tried to move and that was when I realized they were talking about me and the pain, the burning sensation was unbearable. I tried to tell them, but my voice, even to me, sounded like a distant croak. The call of a wounded raven.

'Easy, soldier, don't try to move just yet, your friends are here.' That was McAlpine again.

'Welcome back, Harry Luck.' That was the gentle, soothing voice of Bonnie Luxford.

'I thought for a while there we had lost you, Mr Luck. Welcome home.' Surrette's words.

I drifted back to somewhere far away where it did not hurt, but it was a different kind of darkness and I was no longer afraid.

'He will drift in and out of it for a while yet but each time it will be for longer.' McAlpine again.

'Goodnight, Harry.' Her words whispered in my ear, her lips brushing my temple.

I do not know exactly how long that went on for

because I had no measure of time. Awake, then asleep and then awake again. Sometimes there were people with me and sometimes not. Sometimes it was dark and at others, sunlight shone through the curtains. When there was someone close by, it would be Surrette, Wolf or the doctor but the best times were when Bonnie was there, but somehow those times became less frequent. Then one morning McAlpine came in with Wolf and told me that I could go home. That the Comanche would take care of me, the burns were healing nicely and that it would be better for me to be home than having me forever clogging up one of the only two beds in his establishment. I did not argue.

'Where's Bonnie?' I asked. 'Will she know where to find me?'

Surrette said, 'Her aunt is very ill and she had to take her back to Boston. I'm sure she will be in touch as soon as matters there are sorted. She left you a letter, asked me to give it you when you are on your feet again.'

'A letter?'

'Yes, I have it in the office. I'll get it for you before you leave.' There was something awkward about the man's delivery, but I was concentrating hard on not moving too quickly to worry about it. Any stretching of the repairing skin was painful and would be for some weeks, I was told.

Surrette insisted on driving me back to the Horseshoe in the livery's surrey. It was not a comfortable ride, but neither was it too painful. The best part of it was getting out from under the watchful eye of Doc McAlpine and a freedom to smoke my pipe. We journeyed mostly in silence. There had been no repercussions about our illegal border crossing and the New Mexico Territorial governor had actually thanked Surrette in writing for ridding a few more midnight riders and general border trash from his Territory.

Wolf met us at the door and gently helped me into the cabin. Surrette declined supper, shared a drink with us and climbed back on to the surrey. 'Oh, Mr Luck,' he said, 'I almost forgot to give you this.' He handed me an envelope, smiled and left.

After supper, Wolf said he had some chores to attend to and left me alone with my thoughts and my unopened letter from Bonnie. I sat on the porch with a thick, Indian blanket around my shoulders to keep out the chill of the early winter evening, lit my pipe and carefully opened the letter.

Only it wasn't so much of a letter as a note, the kind you might leave for a neighbour if you were going to be unexpectedly away for a few days and needed someone to feed the chickens. She thanked me for saving her life, hoped I got better soon and said that she would write me when her business in Boston was settled. She signed it simply *gratefully, Bonnie Luxford.* Not exactly the passionate missive I was hoping for, but she probably had a good enough reason for not showing any real emotion. I tried to put my troubled thoughts behind me and concentrated my efforts on building up my strength and getting well. As far as the latter went, Wolf was the ideal man for the job. He quickly disposed of the burn ointments prescribed by Doc McAlpine and replaced them with balms of his own concoction which, although they did not smell as sweet, worked a damned sight better. He explained that the Comanche had learned to deal with burns as a necessity for survival.

CHAPTER NINE

THE FALL

A couple of weeks under his care following my arrival and my health and mobility much improved, we were sitting indoors in front of a roaring fire and well away from the bitter norther that had appeared from out of nowhere with a hint of an early snowfall at its fore. He reached out for my makings and rolled himself his usual fat quirly.

'You ever bought any tobacco in your life, Wolf?' I asked.

'Now why would I do that with friendly folk like you around?'

He had a point, I suppose.

During one long silence, the crackling, wood fire the only illumination inside of the ranch house, I asked, 'How come you talk so fine, Wolf, and didn't have to go to the reservation over in Fort Sill like most of the rest of your people?'

'That's because I am a white man. You cannot send a white man to live on a res.'

I laughed. 'You, a white man? I've never seen a man was more Comanche than you.'

'I have a paper to prove I am a white man. My name is Jacob Brendan Keogh of Michigan.'

'I do not understand,' I said, genuinely puzzled.

'A long way back before your Civil War, there was a big fight out here and most of my village, including my mother and father were killed by soldiers. An infantry major named Brendan Keogh rescued me from our burning tepee. I was only a baby, but I can still smell the stench of the burning hides. He and his wife took me to Michigan and adopted me. He gave me his name and I went to the white man's church and school. I can write, and I am much read. I lived with them until they passed away. Cholera as usual. I was twenty years old and without them felt that I did not belong in Michigan, and so I came home.'

'Home?' I said. 'Canterville was your home?'

'Canterville wasn't here then, just a trading post and stagecoach swing station, but it grew very quickly. An Englishman owned the store and he gave the settlement which later became the town, its name.'

'OK, so why not the res?'

'They tried to put me on the reservation at Fort Sill but failed. I have that paper to prove what I say is true.' He chuckled. 'You want to see it?'

'No thanks, but it is one hell of a story,' I said.

'True stories often are,' he said, then after some thought, 'I'm going to oil that damned windmill tomorrow.'

After three weeks, I was taking gentle rides again and the chestnut was pleased to be under me. On a mild Friday afternoon, I informed Wolf that I was riding into Canterville to collect any mail that may be waiting there for me.

'There wasn't any there on Monday,' he said, his face expressionless.

'Today is another day.'

'True enough. Maybe stay overnight if you are tired, don't overdo it, you are still very weak, although you may not know it. And bring back some tobacco and sugar, we are running low on both.'

'I'll do that,' I said, and walked the horse out of the yard, breaking to a gentle trot when clear of the ranch and out of his sight.

My first call was to the sheriff's office in the county courthouse. Billy Cole was pleased to see me, and I shared a drink with him and an even leaner Joe Prior. I was relieved to note the older man's near-full recovery although it had left him a great deal thinner than I remembered. Billy Cole said, 'Surrette is out of town. It's his harvest time.'

'Oh?' I queried.

'He's out gathering county taxes. He gets a percentage of very dollar he collects, and it isn't easy getting coin out of a hard-up rancher or sodbuster, he seems to make out OK. Be gone a week and we're holding the fort for him.'

I left them there jawing and clicking dominoes, simple enough pleasures, and made my way to the Wells Fargo office which handled the town mail as well as the stage line, telegraph and bank. There were two letters there waiting for me; an official army letter from Fort Laramie and one postmarked Boston, the address written in Bonnie Luxford's neat hand.

I opened the army letter while eating a light supper in the Lucky Black Cat. It was from my old CO, asking me if I would consider re-enlisting under the promoted rank of major. I grunted in appreciation, it was nice to be wanted. I saved Bonnie's letter until after supper then, with a fifth of bourbon in my long coat pocket, I returned to my room.

I opened the letter again and read it, twice.

It said a lot of things about two people having just met who hardly knew each other and yet found an immediate bond and it said a lot of things about death and violence. Yes, Bonnie's note said a lot of things and yet really it said nothing other than goodbye and it only said that once. I folded it neatly and stuffed it inside my pocket. I could retrieve it later, maybe read it a hundred more times, maybe read it until I knew it by heart or it wore out. It was a nothing kind of letter, one for my souvenir box. I took it out of my pocket and read it one more time and then I took a long drink of bourbon and did not stop drinking for seven weeks. I crawled into that bottle and stayed there until the night George Surrette nearly killed a young cowboy for calling me a drunk.

It is not too difficult to become a drunk; you just drink a lot. You crawl into a bottle, any bottle, and you stay there. You don't go home. You take the warm feeling given to you by the alcohol of your choice, enjoying that feeling of warmth, savouring the peace, order and security it brings to your life, so much so that you try to keep it there. Keeping it there is no problem at all so long as you have money to feed the craving, but when your so-called friends, including the local law, separate you from your bank account, quite illegally I believe, life becomes a tad difficult. Now, looking back at my first encounter with Jack Pelham, happily asleep in a filthy bundle of rags in a cold, damp Wells Fargo doorway, it is difficult to understand why such a portent had no meaning for me. I guess it would not have had much impact other than that of revulsion in any passer-by. He was just another tramp and it never really occurred to me until much later as to just how he became the man he was. What plausible reason could a man have to fall so far? I knew not, at least I did not until I became that man.

A man in a doorway, a passing sympathy maybe and four bits in his tin cup, conscience salved.

In some moments, near sober moments, in my decline, asleep in the warm straw of the livery, my presence there tolerated for some reason by the stable man, I thought of Jack Pelham. Lost his wife and two children for no real fault of his own, just a passing disease that claimed souls all over America and especially in the west, where death rode daily alongside the unwary at one time or another. But you must have someone to blame and Jack pointing the finger at himself was a bigger man than me.

I did not meet Jack on my downward spiral. I had heard sometime before the shootout in New Mexico and the subsequent fire at the Horseshoe cabin, that he had sobered up some, pulled himself together and moved to Dallas. He had reached a point that I had not, and I simply took his place in Canterville and when access to my money became impossible, I simply followed in his tracks and mooched money from strangers on both sides of town. Pride was lost to me. I took a swamping job on the Mex side of town, swept out the brothel, the saloons, gambling joints, and picked up any loose change tossed to me by the laughing winners, and sometimes the booted toes of the sore losers.

One time, in the early days of my drunk, Wolf visited me; sat down in a dingy doorway with me from cold sunset to cold sunrise without speaking. As morning came, he got to his feet, nodded and walked away leaving behind him my pipe, a fresh sack of Bull Durham and a pack of matches. On another occasion, in the early hours of a bitterly cold night, a new Surrette deputy, under orders from Surrette I supposed, arrested me for being involved in an alleged fist fight with a drover, an encounter of which I had no recollection. The same part-time deputy brought me a large breakfast the following morning and told me that the drover had dropped any pending assault charges and that I was free to go. I saw Surrette only briefly during that incident and I do not recall a single word passing between us. I should have realized he had just wanted to get me out of the cold and a hot meal inside of me for one night at least. But drunks do not really think about anything other than their own misery and where the next calming drink is coming from.

Mine came from a passing drummer who wrinkled his nose at me, handed me quarter and moved quickly by. I was outside of the Lucky Black Cat and so dry I did not have the energy to walk to one of the seedier saloons below the tracks, a saloon where the barkeep would take my quarter and give me ten minutes to drink it before moving me on. The Lucky Black Cat was a place I had purposefully avoided, but needs must and I badly needed a drink. I pushed my way in through double winter doors, bellied up to the bar close beside a young cowboy, placed my quarter on the polished wood and said to the bartender, 'Whiskey and chaser please, Henry.'

The youngster standing next to me said, 'Jesus H, you stink.'

And so, my long road back from the darkness began. . . .

CHAPTER TEN

WHISKEY RIVER SET ME FREE

Following that confrontation with the young cowboy and George Surrette's ultimatum in the barroom of the Lucky Black Cat, it took me only three weeks to quit the Whiskey River. With the help of the sheriff and the constant and ofttimes irritating company of Wolf, I crawled out on to the bank and I got back into some semblance of a routine. I returned to the Horseshoe and worked hard on restoring the burned cabin. I ate well and only took an occasional glass of Henry's fine wine with an evening meal. I smoked my pipe on the porch and wrote endless letters to Bonnie Luxford at the Boston address Surrette had given to me. They were not letters filled with melancholy, bitterness or the fact that she had left without a proper goodbye, but more often than not, letters filled with my belief in the sheer scope and beauty of the Texas frontier. A place with promise of a real productive future and not of violence and death, just so long as honourable Texans, men like Surrette, were on watch. It would improve and live up to its promise of pleasure and prosperity. Ramblings really, with the paper stained here and there with a tear or two.

I wrote those long letters but never posted them; they stacked up high and unread on the shelf beneath my gunrack and yet, somehow the writing of them eased the pain and helped my recovery and journey back from a very dark place. To aid my redemption I had given myself two distinct goals. One was to repair the cabin and two, to find the men who had ruined my budding dream and to kill them one by one, starting with the man I had shot in the face. He would be the easiest to find and I suspected his companions would not be too far away.

To this end, I practised daily with my Colt, much to the annoyance of Wolf and the local wildlife. Sitting in the glow of the fire one evening, and closely watching me reloading .44.40 calibre rounds, he got to his feet and turned his backside to the burning logs as old men do and said irritably, 'The deer do not come to the yard much now, they are scared you will mistake them for a tin can.'

'I won't harm them,' I said.

'They do not know that.'

'Well you're an Indian and so damned smart, supposed to be a shapeshifter, wind-talker or some damned thing, you tell them.'

'Wind-talkers are Navajo, the Comanche are warriors not shapeshifters.'

'Whatever,' I said, 'I need the practice with the handgun. I find it difficult to hold a rifle to my right shoulder, still tender up around there.'

'Who are you aiming to shoot?'

'Come the early spring I am heading south and right down to Mexico if necessary, then if I can find them, I am going to kill the sonsofbitches who did this to me.'

'Surrette know about this?'

'It is none of the sheriff's business. I am no longer a deputy and he is not my keeper.'

'Are you taking me?'

'Not taking you exactly but if you want to come along, I will be pleased with your company.'

'Are you paying me for that company?'

'I doubt it. I am a little short on money again, at the moment.'

'Then perhaps it would be better we stayed here

and made some money. The beef you ordered will be on the range come spring and they will need you.'

'I have taken care of that. Winkelman and Joe Prior are holding them for me until we return.'

'We?'

'I figured you would want to come along and nursemaid me some more.'

'Why would you figure that?' he asked.

'Well, mostly because you are always fussing over me.'

'I worry about you is all. You have no direction. You smile a lot, but the smile never reaches your eyes. Smiles should light up a person's eyes, your smiles only darken them.'

'And just what the hell would you know about laughter? I don't ever recall you looking much pleased about anything,' I said irritably.

'I have known for a long time this thing you believe in, will please you most but no, the killing of the Comancheros will not be it. What will it be after that? Where are you aiming your soul, in what direction, to what end?'

I got to my feet, poked the fire alive and pushed in three fresh logs. They were dry and crackled, immediately giving off sparks and delivering that sweet scent that only weathered pine logs on an open fire can bring to a room. Our shadows danced on the walls.

'Do you have a direction, Wolf? Do you know where your soul is headed?' I didn't really expect an answer to such a question but I waited just in case.

'Everything in this universe has a soul. The rivers, the mountains, the green valleys, the buffalo, the white-tailed deer, the coyote and even you, Harry Luck, we are all a part of that universe. When my time comes I will travel to the mountains beyond the High Plains, seek out my soul and find Manitou the Great Spirit and join with the everything and the nothing, become part of it for all eternity.'

'Quite a mouthful, but do you really believe that, Wolf? Really believe it, I mean?'

'I want to, so I do.' He addressed his answer as much to the fire as to me.

'I thought you said you went to the white man's church in Michigan.'

'I did and what they believed, the ideas they wanted me to embrace are no stranger or more believable than the beliefs of my people, are they?'

I did not have an answer to that.

'The miracle-working Son of your God dying on a wooden cross and rising from the dead? Is it easier to believe such an idea than it is to accept that you are part of the universe and will return to it when your time here in Texas is done?'

'You may have a point there, sir, you may very

well have.'

He grunted, thought about that for a moment then walked over to the table, picked up the makings and silently left the room.

It was not a hard winter, and spring came sooner to the high country, a long while before it was expected. Wild birds nested early, and the white-tailed deer battled for the young does. The warming sun eased the last of the aches and pains and my burns had healed to white, striped scars. Some were still a little painful and a constant reminder of that day at the cabin when my life was turned around. The fire, Surrette had told me, was not started by the Comancheros, but by Bonnie Luxford herself as she fought off the obvious intentions of her captors and had sent an oil lamp flying, smashing it against the wall and filling the area with kerosene fumes. She had told Surrette that she would prefer to be burned alive than defiled. My arrival had saved her from both.

Billy Coles delivered the chestnut which had overwintered with the Surrette *remuda*, and stayed for coffee and a light supper. He was full of gossip, only a smattering of which I heard but some of it interesting enough for me to listen.

It was election year and George Surrette, he told us, was seriously thinking of retiring and handing the reins over to a younger man. Two local business men had their eye on the job; it could be a lucrative profession in more ways than one. A good lawman could still enhance what was often a meagre salary, with an income from outside interests and yet remain honest. Many gave way to temptation, but no one believed that Surrette was one of them; any coin he made over his county salary was honestly earned. And still he made more than an honest dollar from behind the badge and the many courtesies that went with it.

I was thinking on these things as I cantered the chestnut out of the yard and across the early-morning, breeze-waving grass on the now quite distinct trail to Canterville. My intention was clear. I would try and pick up what was likely to be the very cold trail of the gang. It would take time and a great deal of hard riding, but it was my quest and not to be denied. I no longer pretended it to be a simple case of revenge for the wrong done to Bonnie and harm done to me that day at the cabin. Something inside of me sought penance for the seven-week drunk during which I had probably belittled my friends and traded hard on their friendships. And none more so than upon that of Sheriff George Surrette. I had spoken only briefly with him over the past five weeks and now, fully recovered from both wounds and my swim in the Whiskey River, I was not too sure how he would greet me. I need not have worried. The big man was seated in the padded chair behind his large, polished-wood desk reading a two-day old newspaper. The courthouse was quiet, deserted at that early hour I guessed for lack of need. He looked up from the newspaper and his lips below the shaggy, grey moustache smiled broadly. 'Good Lord, Mr Luck, good to see you looking so fine. Hardly believable, Father Time can sometimes be a bastard but when he is well-intentioned, he surely does a mighty fine job.' He shook my hand, gently at first in case my bravado was hiding any residuals of pain, then, as I returned his grip with my firm one, he laughed and squeezed harder. 'Sit down, take a load off. I've not had breakfast yet.'

'Me neither,' I said, taking the offered chair and settling my backside on to the cold, hard wood.

'We'll put that right directly but first, what brings you to Canterville so early in the day?'

'Two things, Sheriff.'

'Oh, Sheriff business, is it?' Again, the merest hint of a smile at the name routine.

'Mostly,' I said.

'Shoot then. I'm a mite hungry.'

'First off, a big thank you for all that you have done both as a friend and as a lawman. I thank you for your patience and that friendship. I regret it and am sorry if I caused you any embarrassment.'

He waved the words away.

'And secondly, this is a courtesy call to tell you that it is my intent to track down the men who killed the Drago Wells deputy, hurt my friends, and were the indirect cause of burning my house down.

'And Bonnie Luxford?'

'I count her among my friends, both past and present.'

'You are looking to hoe a might big field there, son. You might need to think about it some before you ride a long trail that might not have an end.'

'Every trail has an end one way or another and I've done little else but think on it, both drunk and sober.'

There followed a long and almost painful silence. I felt his grey eyes boring into me, looking for what, I had no idea. Finally, he seemed to reach some conclusion, sighed and tapped the desk top with his long fingers, a drum-roll almost. 'I figured that was what you would be about when fit and ready to ride. You are dead set on this?'

'Yes, I am.'

'Then this may save you some saddle time.' He opened a drawer and withdrew a sheet of paper and handed it to me. It was a Belton County arrest warrant for one Miguel Sanchez.

I looked at him and back at the paper. 'Who is Miguel Sanchez?'

'He's the ugly bastard whose face you did not improve upon. Last seen in the Del Moro region south of the New Mexico line but still this side of the Rio Grande.'

'How do you know that?' I asked.

'I still have contacts down that way. I have not forgotten Drago Wells, Bonnie, or my men. It's what you would call solid intelligence.'

He tossed my old deputy badge on to the desk. 'It will help if you wear that, down there. You will not have any authority once you leave Belton County and Texas, but most other honest lawmen will treat you with courtesy just as I would them. Makes you at least one better than a bounty-hunter.'

'Thanks,' I said, dropping the nickel star into my vest pocket.

'Just remember, Mr Luck, he will not be alone.'

'And neither will I,' I said.

'Wolf?'

I nodded.

'Well I guess he is worth a half dozen Mex bandits, be they Comancheros or just plain miscreants.'

'He sure enough is,' I said. 'Did you know he is a white man?'

He smiled broadly. 'Showed you his bit of paper, I bet.'

We ate a hearty breakfast at the Lucky Black Cat

before I departed for the short ride back to the ranch, his solemn departing words *Voya con dios* gently buzzing in my ears.

CHAPTER ELEVEN

THE TEXAS RANGERS

I spent that last Sunday on the Horseshoe securing the buildings. I did not wish for a marauding, hungry, black bear emerging from his winter's sleep, coming down off the mountain and destroying weeks of hard labour. Perhaps I should have gone to church, but I had said my goodbyes to Surrette and did not want to prolong the departure. Wolf cooked a fine supper for us and we shared a cigar on the porch, sitting there in relative silence. We stayed well into the late evening, listening to the night sounds, a mating fox in the distance and the cry of an owl on the hunt for the unwary spring-born rabbit on the fringe of the treeline. And always, day or night, the soft sound of the wind in the trees or brushing through the long grass below us.

I must admit that I enjoyed such evenings with the taciturn old Comanche, an unspoken appreciation of the wilderness around us and both, in our separate ways bent on preserving it. I wanted more people, he wanted fewer. I wanted to see more children in the new schoolhouse, recently built on Banner Street where it crossed Main Street by the courthouse. He was worried that people would eventually destroy the place and, in more sombre moments, told me he was happy in many ways that he was an old man and would not live to see the changes, be they good or bad. That made me smile. The old bastard had more energy in him than I ever had, albeit he expended it at a much slower and more graceful pace. I insisted that all the time we had men like Surrette keeping watch, that would never happen. I doubt that my words reassured him in any way, but we seldom chewed long over it one way or the other. I told him we would ride at sunup after an early breakfast, and to have the horses ready.

I did not sleep well that night. Dark and yet firelit visions of Bonnie lying in my arms in the dirt outside of the cabin, filled the shadows of my room and once, briefly, I fancied she was there beside me telling me it was all right, things would be good again one day. Even as she spoke, a huge, ugly bucktoothed man, part Yaqui and part Mexican, leapt from my spiralling thoughts, his cheeks bloody, his lips spitting blood and broken teeth all over us. I tried for my Colt, but my hand was on fire and before I could pull the weapon he had vanished amid a dark mist that became my morning. I gave up on sleep, climbed out of bed and prepared breakfast which was ready just as the pale sun promised to rise above the eastern horizon and give me another day. Wolf must have smelt the bacon. He was standing in the yard. I hardly recognized him. He was dressed in dark-blue wool pants, plaid green shirt, a grey vest and long, buckskin-fringed jacket, the kind favoured by the showman Bill Cody. He had retained his moccasin boots, lost his feathered headband and replaced it with a black, flat, wide-brimmed, high-rounded crown, reservation hat.

I stared at him and then at the buckskin horse standing saddled by the chestnut.

'What's the matter?' he asked. 'It's my disguise. We might be going places they don't like Comanches.'

'And the horse?' I asked, thinking of nothing else to say.

'Couldn't paint the pony all over so got a new one from Surrette, all on your account in place of wages. Thanks.'

'You're very welcome,' I said, inwardly smiling, thinking it was some disguise. He looked a sight bigger in the new clothes and younger but he still looked all Comanche to me and I guessed people might think twice about tangling with us, even south of the border.

We rode from the yard and I did not look back; I had been looking back too often those last few weeks and now it was time to look to the task ahead. The desire for revenge had lessened, replaced with a need for justice. Perhaps that was why Surrette had insisted on the warrant and the badge. A curbing rein, a hobble on my anger which had also dissipated.

We headed south and skirted around Canterville, south but always leaning a little to the west in the general direction of the border country around Del Moro. I had reckoned it would take several days of easy riding to reach the border and that our progress would be slowed by questions that needed to be asked and intelligence gathered. Surrette had told me over breakfast that last morning in Canterville that the local town marshal of a small hamlet called Abbotsville, was an old friend, Ben Jardine, and the man who had given him the information on Miguel Sanchez, so that seemed a likely place to make as a first stop.

Just as dusk was falling with a promise of rain in

the air and a chilly mist wrapping itself around the countryside, we rode into the yard of a small, but sturdy homestead and waited by the gate, as was the custom, to be invited to step down and water the horses. It was our second night on the trail. The light inside the cabin was extinguished and the door of the timber-built cabin opened. A small, bearded man in faded and worn, blue dungarees stepped out of the darkened cabin cradling a double-barrelled shotgun in the crook of his arm. He stared at us from under the floppy brim of his sweat-stained hat. A hat that was so battered it made my worn campaign hat look like new. He studied on us for a long moment. 'What can I do you fellows for?' he asked in a thin, reedy voice.

'We would like to water the horses and maybe shelter in your barn for the night. It looks like rain.'

He studied on us some more, paying particular attention to Wolf.

I opened my jacket so that he could see the star pinned to my vest. 'Deputy out of Canterville. We are on Belton County business.'

'This ain't Belton and you are one long ways off your patch.' He did not take his eyes from Wolf. 'He a deputy too?'

'And his horse,' I said, 'county employees both.'

'You are welcome to the barn but not the Indian.'

'Excuse me?' I said.

'No Goddamned savage is sleeping in my barn. I got kids inside the house.'

'He's not hungry,' I said. 'He ate already.'

'Don't smart mouth me, son, deputy or no deputy, no Indian is getting near my family. You can water your animals and get gone.' He raised the double-barrels slightly higher. 'Don't look at me like you are better than me neither.' He pulled off his hat revealing a bald, ragged scar from the hairline to the crown.

I looked at Wolf.

'And don't look at me neither, Harry, I didn't do it.' It was the first time he had ever called me by my given name. He smiled, touched the brim of his big hat and walked his horse to the water tank, stepping down to fill his canteen from the pump, remounting and riding out of the yard to be quickly swallowed by the growing darkness.

'I think you hurt his feelings some,' I said, as I turned my horse to the tank, let the chestnut drink its fill, topped up my canteen and climbed back up on to the already cold saddle. 'The town of Canterville thanks you, Texas thanks you and I thank you for your hospitality, sir,' I said quietly as I swung the chestnut around and followed the buckskin out and into the night. My anger at his attitude had been minimised by Wolf's humour and memories of my own innermost feelings when the burn scars on my back and leg had ached fit to make me weep.

Most of the terrain we traversed was grass-covered and featureless, much like the Llano Estacado, the staked plains along the western edge of the state and far to the north of us. But here there were no pioneer-driven marker stakes in the ground to show where the trail should be. I was glad I had brought along my army compass, although Wolf had little faith in it and twice showed us a better route up to the higher ground where the ravens flew, and the grey rocks of the escarpment showed us we were near to the border with New Mexico.

On that fourth night out and a day after our run-in with the unfriendly homesteader, we approached a wooded clearing. It was a clear, moonlit night, the first clear night when you could actually see the stars, including, I supposed, the one that adorned our flag and was somewhere up there shining down on Texas. Strange how quickly I had assumed the identity of a Texan. I could smell wood-smoke and Wolf hung back a little, his Henry drawn and across his knees. The campfire was flickering low and I could see the silhouettes of four horses tied to a string between two small trees.

We reined in our horses and I yelled, 'Hello the camp, two riders coming in.'

'Show yourselves then and keep your hands

clear of any firearms.' A voice from the darkness.

I nodded to Wolf who returned the Henry to its scabbard as we walked the horses forward.

A tall man in a long, grey duster stepped out of the shadows. He had a Winchester cradled in his arms and his hat was pulled low over his face. He had a soft, almost relaxed, Texas drawl, a young man's voice. 'Can I help you boys?'

'Saw the fire, smelt the coffee, that speaks for itself out here I would have thought,' I said, lightly.

'That depends, mister. Matt, you there? I'm going forward,' he called over his shoulder.

'Right here, brother.' A voice in the darkness.

The young man lowered the carbine and stepped nearer, looking up at us, from me to Wolf and then back again. I could clearly see the silver star set in a circle and forged from a Mexican five-peso piece, pinned to his breast as the duster fell open, I assumed, quite deliberately. 'Where you boys headed?'

'Del Moro,' I said. The chestnut fidgeted at the smell of the tethered horses; she was a gregarious animal, always wanting to be friendly. The young man stepped nearer and stroked her muzzle, she snorted and nudged his hand when he stopped. A Texas Ranger now but a one-time horse wrangler I would bet.

'What business do you have there?'

I let my own duster fall open so that he could

make out my badge in the moonlight. 'Sheriff's Deputies out of Canterville, Belton County. We're on the hunt.'

'You are some long ways out of Canterville and your jurisdiction, my friend.'

'Yes, we have already been told that. It makes no never mind though. I have paper on a man and I mean to serve it on him one way or another.' I kept my voice friendly but my tone firm.

'Sounds like personal business, is it?'

'You could say that.'

'May I see the warrant?'

I fished it out of my pocket and handed it down to him. He held it up and read it from the moon and fire's combined glow, then carefully refolded it and handed it back to me. He tipped his hat on to the back of his shaggy head and smiled. There was a genuine warmth to it. 'I know George Surrette, we call him Crusty Surrette down here. Solid as gold, a miserable old bastard and cantankerous as all hell. The Indian with the county?'

'Yes, the Comanche tracker is also on the county payroll; he is also a miserable bastard, cranky and cantankerous as all hell but I trust my life with him as does Surrette.'

'Welcome to you both then, ride on in.' He turned toward the fire and yelled, 'They are coming in boys, all's good.'

There were four of them, old men in young

men's bodies.

The young ranger held out his hand. 'Sergeant Luke Billings, these are my brothers Matthew and Mark. The kid over there by the fire is Charlie Moyes; we are part of C Company riding out of Fort Worth.'

I studied on the three brothers, alike as peas in a pod, their age difference barely discernible. 'Your mother must have popped you three out pretty close together.'

'One for every year. We were born within sight of the Marfa lights, Daddy thought those spooky mountain lights were the restless souls of dead Rangers. He also thought he was Mark Twain.' He laughed at a happy memory.

'Harry Luck,' I said. 'Belton County deputy riding out of Canterville and this is Wolf Keogh, my tracker.'

We dismounted, and a young man stepped forward, took the bridles and led the horses away. I shook hands all round although Wolf just waved and moved to a seat on a log set in a shadowy spot but nearest the lee side of the fire. He rolled a cigarette and I lit my pipe as we drank their coffee. Five lawmen and a Comanche at ease in the moonlight, things can never be much better than this, I thought to myself, quite suddenly missing the general camaraderie of the men of the Fort Laramie garrison.

Young Moyes could not take his eyes from Wolf, watching his every move. He looked away for a moment and asked, 'Sir, is he a tame Comanch'?'

He was not old enough to have been involved in the bloody and violent confrontation between the Indians and the Texas Rangers of the Comanche War but had probably had an earful of lurid tales from older rangers. I looked over at a smiling Luke Billings, winked and said, 'He's placid enough now, son, but I would not try to hand feed him were I you.'

The boy looked relieved, then over at the unsmiling Wolf and asked hopefully, 'Do you have a spare smoke, old man? We are out of tobacco.'

Wolf got to his feet, went to his saddle-bag and extracted a fresh sack of Durham, tossing it to the young ranger. 'Keep it, we got plenty.' He looked at me. 'Courtesy of Wolf Keogh.' He emphasized the 'Keogh' for my benefit I thought, gave me an odd look and returned to his seat in the shadows, watching as they passed the sack around.

Luke addressed me directly and said, 'In case you are wondering, there was a brother, John. He was shot and killed by a one-eyed Irishman at Casey Junction, a one-horse town just north of Del Rio. The man was wanted for murdering his wife. John went down going forward and took his man down with him. We left the Irishman to rot and took John back to Fort Worth.'

'That must have been hard to take,' I offered.

'Line of duty, we don't sign on to die but we know it can happen. We were brought up Rangers. Where is your man, this Sanchez at?'

'Down around Del Moro ways.'

'That's way over the border, down along the Pecos River. We don't venture that way unless in pursuit. It's election year and both governors are a bit fidgety at this time. My ass would be in a sling were I to help you and I am sorry about that.'

'Not to worry. What are you doing in this neck of the woods anyway?'

'Six cons, lifers, busted out of the Del Rio jail. They were in transit for the state pen, they broke out, killed two guards and an old man and his dog just for the hell of it, cleared out most of the jail armoury and fled. It's really a case for the US Marshals office but we help each other out from time to time.'

'You know where they are?'

'We do. They are holed up in an abandoned soddy, two miles from here. It's beside a small creek and we aim to hit them early in the morning just after first light, maybe catch one of them going to the privy, lower the odds a little.' He hesitated. 'If you want to help you would be most welcome but it's up to you.'

I looked over at Wolf, he nodded, and I said yes, and to count us in.

Luke took out his watch and leaned nearer to the firelight. 'Best we turn in then, we have an early start, it will be a cold breakfast, but we can eat when the job is done.' He sounded very confident, filled with the enthusiasm of the adventurous young. Being a little more circumspect, I just hoped we would all still be alive to enjoy that breakfast.

We were in position long before first light. All four sides of the soddy were covered. Wolf was the gun on the high ground at my recommendation as to his prowess with the Henry Rifle. I was the lowest and nearest to the cabin where I could effectively use my Colt, having explained that a shoulder injury hampered my use of a long gun. The young Luke Billings did not enquire as the origins of the wound and I offered no explanation other than to say it was a healing injury.

Just as the sun peeped over the eastern horizon, giving light to what in other times would have been an idyllic vista, smoke drifted out of the soddy's chimney and moments later the door opened and a tall man in the ragged remains of a prison uniform, his braces dangling, made his way across the rutted ground to a single-seater privy on the left of the building. Without warning, one of the rangers, I could not tell which, opened fire and missed with his first round but hit with the second as the man dodged to one side and ran for the cover of the rocks by the creek, the shot spilling the fugitive into the shallow water. There were yells of confusion from within the soddy and the air became very lively around me as a hail of fire was laid around the rock behind which I was sheltering, and one man ran out of the doorway, firing wildly. I dropped him with a single round and ducked back down as the men inside of the soddy marked from where my shot had come.

'Cease fire, men,' the young ranger yelled above the din. 'We'll give them a chance to come out with their hands up. You in the cabin, you hear what I am saying? This is C Company of the Texas Rangers out of Fort Worth and you are surrounded.'

His enquiry was met by a fusillade as the combatants in the cabin thought they had located his position. We held our fire and waited. During the lull, I guessed the besieged outlaws were reloading, Billings yelled out again. 'I'm taking that as a big no, boys, so pour it in on them,' and we did. I have no idea as to how many rounds we fired but I emptied the Colt three times and Wolf's Henry must have been red hot.

'Hold your fire.' Again, from the young sergeant, then he broke cover and on a fast run zig zagging to the bullet-riddled cabin door, kicking it in and rushing inside, revolver in hand; it was a foolhardy move at best but he was lucky. Two close-fired rounds and he stepped back out into the early morning light and waved his smoking revolver at us.

The inside of the cabin was a mess of blood, splintered timber, broken glass, and shot-up furniture. The four bodies were strewn about the place, their dirty, striped suits covered in blood, each man having taken at least half a dozen rounds. It was hard to imagine the hell in that single living space, created by our solid wall of gunfire.

We buried all six of them in shallow graves quickly dug and filled in the sandy ground a hundred or so yards from the creek, stuck a roughly-made cross over each grave and then returned to the cabin to eat their left-over and remarkably undamaged victuals of bacon and eggs prepared by Wolf. We ate outside in the fresh air, kneeling close by the creek, enjoying the warmth of the sun, happy to be alive.

Shortly before noon we bade the young rangers goodbye. Luke Billings said he would wire Surrette and advise him of our whereabouts and of the assistance we had given him. They headed back to Fort Worth and we set out for Abbotsville, Del Moro County, New Mexico.

CHAPTER TWELVE

ABBOTSVILLE

Abbotsville was about what I had expected, a one street town consisting of little more than a saloon, a hotel, several lodging houses, a barber's shop and general store with a livery stable out back. The striped pole had a neatly-lettered sign beside it advising anyone interested that it doubled as an undertaker's establishment, the word establishment was misspelt. The only real anomaly was the telegraph office which appeared to double as a post office and I wondered if either did much business. It was a no-account town, too small to warrant a Del Moro County deputy and the townspeople had apparently, according to Surrette, gotten together to hire an over-the-hill old lawman as town constable and he had improved that title somewhat by elevating it to that of town marshal. It was a stopping place for weary travellers and a shelter of sorts for washed-up cowboys out of work and out of luck. The one building a little above the rest, as far as a coat of paint was concerned, sported the shingle of Marshal's Office and that is where we headed, tying our weary horses off at the rickety hitching- rail after first watering them at the single trough in front of the hotel aptly named The Rider's Rest. We paused on the sidewalk to shed our dusters and beat a lot of the county from our hats before going inside. As I reached for the iron door latch a voice called out and I turned to see a bent, old stick of a man waving at us and crossing the rutted street in our direction. He was a weathered stump of a man as bowed, brown and wrinkled as I have ever seen. The lower half of his tanned face almost hidden by a large, drooping, grey moustache. His frayed, black, town suit hung around his shoulders, only fitting where it touched. His pants were wrinkled and a little short of the tops of his elastic-sided boots. There was a shield hanging on the oversized vest and if he was wearing a firearm, I could not see it.

'You fellows looking for me?' His voice sounded as if it were coming from somewhere deep inside and bore no relation to his general appearance. It was firm and clear, tobacco tainted, clearly phrased without accent of any kind. An educated voice clear and sharp as were his dark eyes studying us from beneath the brim of a dusty derby hat that leaked grey hair. He somehow reminded me of a smaller and much older George Surrette.

He stopped in front of us, giving Wolf the full treatment before turning to me and reading the Canterville-issue deputy's badge. He nodded. 'George sent you I guess, wired he was sending someone. You must be Harry Luck.' He turned to Wolf. 'And this gentleman would be?'

'Wolf Keogh, he also works for Canterville sheriff's office, he's my tracker.'

'Pretty damned good at it too, I'll bet.'

'The best in the business,' I said.

'Well that's good, Ben Jardine does not hold race, the chosen religion or political persuasion no matter how misguided it may be, even if it be republican, against any man. Your companion is as welcome here as you are, and you are Goddamned mightily welcome. I have not seen a strange face or heard a strange voice in a donkey's age. Damned quiet time of the year in Del Moro County give or take a renegade killing or two and I guess that's the reason you are both here. Come inside, have a glass of the good stuff and not that dirt water they sell in the Raven Saloon. Not too early for a snort, is it?'

'It's late in the day somewhere,' I said.

'You're damned right it is,' he said.

His office was clean and tidy and sparsely furnished with a large desk, a couple of chairs, a bench, gunrack and unlit potbellied stove. I could see a single, iron-bar cell leading off from the office but that was it. He quickly produced three glasses and a bottle from a desk drawer and poured three generous shots of what turned out to be a fine bourbon. I nodded my approval. 'George sent me a half case of the stuff. My guess is it was to oil the wheels for your arrival but there was really no need for that.' He gave a big grin that wiggled the moustache. 'But that does not mean I cannot enjoy it. Your health, gentlemen and confusion to your enemies.' We raised our glasses. It was my first drink of strong alcohol in a long while and the first spirit I had ever seen Wolf accept. The Comanche looked at me, a hint of concern in his eyes but I nodded reassuringly and noted that the exchange was not missed by Ben Jardine.

'Abbotsville is usually pretty quiet except on these Saturday nights. Then we get folk in from all over, break the boredom, take a drink, chew the fat, listen to music; we have a fair piano player and some fine voices, including my own. Do either of you sing?' Wolf gave his best bland face, smiled and walked out into the sunshine, saying he would take care of the horses while I practised.

'I guess not then,' Jardine said, looking a little disappointed at the response to his question. 'And you, Deputy Luck, do you sing?'

'Not even for my supper,' I said, 'but I am a good listener.'

'Then I'll see you in the Raven around eight and I will bring the good stuff.' He tapped the bottle. 'I suggest you register at The Rider's Rest, not stately but clean and the food is reasonable. Also, you may find we have a visitor or two who might well be of interest to you in the saloon tonight. I don't believe Miguel Sanchez to be very far from here, down by the Pecos River most likely and some of his acquaintances may pay us a visit.'

'That would be kind of convenient,' I said, bidding him good afternoon and heading for the livery to pick up Wolf and register in the only hotel in town.

The desk clerk was a little hesitant when he turned the register for me to sign and with some disapproval as I passed it on to Wolf, but he noted my badge and kept his mouth tightly shut. The room was a tad small for a pair of grown men, but the two beds were clean and there were fresh towels by the wash basin. It was not stately, as Jardine had said, but I thought it to be a comfortable change from the hard rock beds we had endured for the past few nights. Wolf was not impressed and opted to sleep in the loft above the livery and I did not try to dissuade him. After all, beneath his new clothes he was still a full-blooded

Comanche and would likely find it to be uncomfortable sharing a room.

Alone, I washed, shaved and changed into a clean shirt. I did not know if the hotel ran to a laundry service and made a mental note to enquire. I cleaned and oiled my Army Colt revolver and extended that oiling to the inside of the holster. Chores all done, I stretched out on the bed and thought about Wolf's troubled look when I downed the bourbon. He need not have worried. The smooth, sweet taste of the liquor only served as a bitter reminder of something I wanted to forget. Introspectively, I hoped that there would always be something or someone there to bring to life the memories of my self-inflicted misery. It was no one's fault other than my own, that I took that downward spiral and certainly not Bonnie Luxford's. She owed me nothing, she was right, we hardly knew each other. No promises were ever exchanged, I made my own bed and did not have the willpower or the strength to sleep in it was all. That had changed, partly because of the trail Wolf and I had taken, but mostly because I realized my own worth and the value of the trust my relatively-new friends in Canterville had placed upon me. Perhaps a man should be loyal to something other than himself; some may choose a country, a flag or a religion but, counter to my own beliefs, I chose me. Loyalty to one's own self, if honourable, can only serve to reflect loyalty in others. Fanciful thoughts in a six-bit room in the two-bit town of Abbotsville, New Mexico Territory, as I drifted off to sleep, sinking a little deeper into the soft, thick mattress.

The jingle jangle of a hot, slightly out of tune piano woke me. It was dark outside, only the flickering of a handful of kerosene lamps eased the darkness away. I looked out of the window over Main Street and was surprised to see so many horses along the hitching rails, and even a sprinkling of buggies including one grand Surrey. I was hungry, I washed the sleep from my eyes and, after giving it much thought, I strapped on my sidearm and made my way down to the hotel's small dining room and ordered a well-done steak. It came with baked potatoes and green beans. It was a common enough meal but more than passably well-cooked. After washing it down with a glass of warm beer, I made my way out on to the street, wondering where Wolf was holed up. He wasn't. He was on the sidewalk sitting on a round-backed chair a little to the left of the hotel doorway and looked up at my approach.

'Have you eaten yet?' I asked.

'Later,' he said.

'Have you been sitting there long?'

'Most of the afternoon.'

'Why?'

'It irritates the hell out of the desk clerk,' he growled.

I shook my head in wonder. 'I'm going over to meet Jardine. We'll see who turns up. Are you coming?'

'I'll join you in a little while, this is more fun and besides, that piano is out of tune. Going to be a long evening waiting for nothing to happen.'

I left him sitting there, the hint of a smile on his craggy face. Comanches, old Comanches, go figure, I thought to myself.

The inside of the Raven was just like a thousand other small saloons across the west. A long bar backed by a cracked mirror, an odd assortment of scattered tables and chairs with a small stage at one end. The bar was smooth and polished and there were two bartenders on duty. Both were cast from the same mould, long aprons, striped vests, moustachioed pale faces and slicked-back hair. A waiter carrying trays, dodged his way between the tables. Jardine was seated at a table on his own, his back to the wall lawman-style and with an empty chair in front of him. He saw me and waved me over.

I carefully made my way across to him and sat on the vacant chair. Slightly uncomfortable at having my back to the room, I moved it around so that we were side by side. He nodded approvingly and said, 'I bet Bill Hickock would have wished he had done just that.'

Referring to the fact that the Deadwood lawman had not protected his back and died because of it. 'Bourbon?' he asked, producing a fat hip flask.

'No thanks, not tonight, but thanks all the same.' I signalled the busy waiter over and ordered a beer.

'Put it on my bill, Jonny,' Jardine said, and I wonder if he ever paid a bar bill. It was his town.

I sipped the warm beer, noting it was mostly a frothy head. 'Anyone in tonight would be of interest to me, Marshal?'

'Yes, Mr Luck, as a matter of fact there is maybe three of them, they came in just ahead of you, standing at the end of the bar, greasy bastards.'

Three armed men, Mexican or maybe of mixed race, a trace of Yaqui in the oldest of the three. A short, stocky, swarthy-faced man in a waisted, fancy, gold-braided jacket, cord pants, large, roweled spurs, a pistol on one hip and a large bowie knife on the other. He was about forty, forty-five years of age, with a full head of dark hair, a drooping moustache and a large, fancy sombrero hanging by its chinstrap down his broad back. His companions were similarly attired but less flamboyantly so in their drab, regular working clothes.

'And why would he be of interest to me?'

'That's Jorge Emilio Palmas. He has been known to ride with Miguel Sanchez; where one is, the other will not be too far away. He hasn't been seen in Abbotsville for some weeks now, so you just might be in luck, sir.'

'Luck by name, Lucky by nature,' I said, sipping the beer and studying the man over the rim the glass. I watched him for over an hour. At just before midnight his two companions, both a little unsteady on their feet, left him drinking alone at the bar and made their way out of the saloon. I looked at Wolf who had just joined us, finally tired of baiting the little desk clerk. 'We want that man alone and without a fuss, can you handle that?'

'Where do you want him?'

I looked at Jardine. 'Can I use your jail cell for a couple of days, no questions asked?'

'Just so long as I can watch and learn,' he said, with a worrying eagerness.

'The cell it is then,' I said. 'Do you want any help, Wolf?'

'No, he's such a little man, he will be in the cell by first light, count on it.'

CHAPTER THIRTEEN

A TEXAS WOLVERINE

The first person the dazed Jorge Emilio Palmas saw when he awoke on Sunday morning, his face sporting a black eye and a badly-bruised cheek, was me staring at him through the iron bars of the single Abbotsville jail cell. He tried to get to his feet but suddenly realized his legs were in irons and his hands firmly shackled to an iron wall ring. 'What the hell?' he said, an edge of panic in his high-pitched, deeply-accented voice. 'What the hell goes on here? What did I do?'

'Nothing yet, *amigo,*' I answered in the warmest and friendliest voice I could muster. 'It's a matter of what you do next and then what will happen if that is not to my liking.'

'And who the hell are you?'

'I'm a deputy sheriff out of Belton County, Canterville, to be exact. Do you remember Belton County?'

'I've never been to Belton or Canterville, never even heard of such places. You got the wrong man, *hombre*, I swear it.'

I took the warrant out of my jacket pocket and pretended to read it. 'You are Miguel Sanchez, are you not?'

'No, sir, I'm Jorge Emilio Palmas, ask anyone.' There was relief in his tone and he relaxed back on to the bunk.

'But you know of this Sanchez, am I right?'

'Sanchez is a pretty common name down here as is Miguel. We're damn near in Mexico.'

'Do you mind telling me where he is at, this Miguel Sanchez?'

'Like I said, deputy, I don't know the man.'

'Wrong answer and not to my liking. You have a choice here this morning, Jorge Emilio Palmas,' I said, folding up the warrant and returning it to my pocket. 'You can walk out of here in a couple of days a free man or you can die here today, the choice is yours, all you have to do is give me the answer I want to the question I asked. Where is Miguel Sanchez hiding out?'

'Gringo, you know what? You can go to Hell.'

I gave a great snort of a sigh and turned to Wolf and Jardine who were standing behind me, out of view of the cell, and said to Jardine, 'Looks like we are going to have to do this the hard way, Marshal Jardine.'

Both men stepped forward and gave Palmas the eye.

Palmas looked from one to the other. 'What's he doing here?' The little man was obviously alarmed at the sight of the big Comanche.

I ignored the question and asked one of my own. 'Marshal, do you know of anyone hereabouts might have a wolverine I could hire, preferably a small one?'

Jardine gave it a long minute's thought and said, 'Uncommon this far south but Billy Hayes caught a young one up on the high range a week or so ago. He was going to make a pet of it but it bit his thumb off.'

'Does he still have it?' I asked.

'I doubt it, it was all chewed up and bloody, you know what those critters can do to a man's thumb if he's not too careful.'

'Not his thumb, Marshal, the wolverine.'

'Oh, I think he still has that.'

I took a silver dollar out of my vest pocket and gave it him. 'Hire the damned weasel for me. He can have it back later and get a dollar more when I'm done with it. Take Wolf, here, with you, he can wrangle the thing. Put it in a gunny sack and bring it here directly.'

The two old men left without a word and I returned to my seat in front of the cell and rolled a cigarette. I tipped the chair back against the wall, my hat low over my eyes, and waited for the inevitable question. It didn't take long in coming.

'Hey, what you want the wolverine for, Sheriff?'

I did not answer right away. He needed to sweat.

'You hear me, Sheriff?'

'Deputy,' I said. 'I'm a deputy sheriff.' I waited some more.

'What you going to do with a wolverine in here, man?'

'You answer my question, Jorge, then, nothing. You don't answer it though, and that gunny sack with one very angry little wolverine in it is going over your head until you do. And if you still refuse me, it will no doubt chew your face off.' Before I could go into more detail, Wolf and Jardine returned. Jardine looked worried and was holding a bloodied rag around his left hand and Wolf was toting a large gunny sack with a writhing, spitting, squealing critter in it.

'Time's up, Jorge,' I said, taking the writhing sack from Wolf and moving toward the cell door.

'Wait, wait up,' he sobbed and backed as far away from the door as the chain would allow. 'Get me paper, I'll draw you a damned map, just keep that thing away from me, get it out of my sight, for God's sake, take it away.' He smelt bad, sweat was pouring down his face and his eyes were tear-filled. I have never seen a man so frightened, not even in the war.

Jardine studied on the map Palmas had drawn with a trembling hand while shifting his gaze constantly from the paper to the noisy and still-writhing sack on Jardine's desk. His scrawl showing a small section of the Pecos River about ten miles south of Abbotsville, confirming the location of a small, adobe village just over the border with New Mexico.

Jardine said, 'Looks right, he might not still be there of course, but it is off the beaten track, a safe bet and a good hideaway. I strayed across the line there one-time out hunting; there is a small cantina as I recall, but not a mission. Mostly dirt-poor farmers, peons.'

'OK then,' I said. 'We will go with that, but will need some sort of a battle plan. We will be out-numbered but will have surprise on our side. I'll work on it.'

'Outnumbered?' Jardine said. 'That's a mighty big understatement, there's only three of us.'

'You don't have to ride with us, Ben, you've done your bit.'

'The hell I have. I can take a buggy most of the

way and ride the last mile or two. I'm old but I'm not dead yet and this badge means something to me.'

'Thanks,' I said. What else was there to say but thanks when a man you hardly know offers to risk his life for you?

'What shall I do with the critter?' Wolf asked.

'He's earned his freedom, let him loose out back. Big fellow, is he?'

'Biggest we could find.'

He opened the back door and turned the sack upside down, pouring out a scruffy and somewhat bemused ginger cat, which meowed, took a quick look around and dived beneath the opposite building.

Palmas burst in to tears and made a hasty verbal judgement as to our parentage.

Jardine unwrapped the bloody bandage, wiped the ketchup off his hand and said, 'That's what you really call letting the cat out of the bag.' I smiled, but I think the remark may have been lost on Wolf, although you never could tell with that old man.

I wished we had more information about the village, and was still leaning over the map the following morning when there was a knock on my hotel room door. I picked up my Colt, knowing it would not be Wolf. He would barge straight in, and I cautiously opened the door. 'What the hell are you doing here?' was my rude greeting to the smiling Sergeant Henry Billings shadowed by the young Charlie Moyes.

'Not too sure,' he said, 'but whatever you say is OK with us. We're on furlough.'

The two of them in their long, grey, bulky dusters and both carrying rifles, just about filled the little room. 'Sit anywhere you can find,' I said, pushing forward the two chairs, seating myself down on one of the beds.

'We seen Mr Wolf downstairs,' Charlie Moyes said, 'And he filled us in on the wolverine, but apart from that he's a little short on words.'

'What are you doing this far west?' I asked, puzzled.

'Well, I wired your boss to tell him where you were at and thanked him for your support. He wired my boss and my boss wired your boss' boss and so here we are. No badges, simply courtesy support should it be needed if you cross the New Mexico border.'

'Is that how it works?' I shook my head and realized I had been doing that a lot of late.

'There's more.'

'What, you called out the 6th Cavalry as well?'

'Almost as good as that. George Surrette will be here first thing in the morning, coming part way by train and the last forty miles by horse. A hot ride but not a hard one. He'll be crusty, sure enough though.

You ever seen that good old boy in a gunfight?'

'Twice,' I said, unable to hide the smile, 'and both times he got himself shot.'

'He walked away though.'

'Limped more like it,' I said.

'You have any more Comanche coming?' Wolf said, pushing his way into the room and catching the last bit of Henry Billing's explanation.

'No sir, Mr Wolf, you are the only one we need,' Charlie Moyes said, laughing.

Much of the following morning was wasted jawing and awaiting the arrival of George Surrette. He arrived a little after noon and, as Billings had predicted, he was hot, weary and very cranky, but after a beer and a long talk with his old friend Ben Jardine, a cursory acknowledgement of me, he became approachable enough to sit down and air his thoughts on the situation.

We had moved to the hotel dining room and Jardine had cleared one of the larger tables of cloth and cutlery and advised the hotelier we were not to be disturbed.

'The way I see it,' Surrette opened, 'is that we should not be over there. It's New Mexico Territory and although we have been given a nod, that's all it is, a nod. Things turn sour, we will be left high and dry and likely out of work. So,' he paused for effect, 'we need to be in and out very quickly and we all need to get out, no one left behind in New Mexico, dead or alive. These are mostly Comancheros and we don't know how many of them there are. We need to have a rough idea and I suggest Wolf go take a looksee, and based on any intelligence gathered, we plan from that point, not from the here and now, totally blind as to the odds. It hurts to say this but, if the odds are too high, we back off and get on with our lives. I want Miguel Sanchez but not at any cost and chances are, sooner or later he will be back in Texas and we will get another shot.'

There was a long silence, my army experience told me he was right as his Ranger experience did so for Henry Billings. Whatever we needed to decide upon was down to Wolf, and he had already left, even as Surrette had said what was needed of him. Wolf was not big on words as young Moyes had already observed.

We idled the rest of the afternoon and evening away as best we could. Surrette and Jardine talked about old times, the two rangers took several of the locals for a dollar or two at the Raven's poker table and I sipped beers on Jardine's credit. The old marshal had shed a lot of years in the hours we had been in Abbotsville and I wondered if that was what old age was really all about; keeping alive was being alive and enthusiasm for the task ahead had straightened his back and put a fire in his eyes.

I shared a few hands of poker and another pair

of beers before saying goodnight and retiring to my room. I sat at the small bureau and wrote another letter to Bonnie Luxford, telling her she was always in my thoughts and that when this quest was over I would most likely be selling the Horseshoe and re-joining my old command at Fort Laramie. I did not know if that was true, but it was an option that was appealing to me more and more with each day that passed. The reason for that, I believed, was that the Horseshoe could never be a home to me without her there by my side. Like Jardine, perhaps I too was getting old and needing more than the fine yesterdays behind me, in order to face all the uncertain tomorrows.

I folded the letter carefully and put it in my inside jacket pocket. Should I be killed, I hoped it would be Surrette or Wolf who would find it.

CHAPTER FOURTEEN

A TEXAS HELLO

Wolf reported back a little after first light with the information we needed. The village consisted of a wide, main, hardpacked thoroughfare with dwellings mostly on one side and on the other a cantina and storage buildings. He estimated, accurately he assured us, that there were up to fourteen Comancheros there including Jorge Emilio Palmas, which brought a bitter tirade from Jardine. It was news to him that the outlaw was no longer in his cell, but the old Mexican jailer was. He suspected bribery but there was little to be done about it. It simply meant that Sanchez would know we were coming, but not how many of us. That information would have depended on when Palmas was released. Numbers aside though, he would be ready. Jardine suggested that it was quite possible the gang would flee south, but both Surrette and I thought that to be unlikely. They were far superior in number and were probably tired and unhappy with being on the run from a Texas sheriff's deputy.

We were once again seated in the hotel dining room, drinking hot coffee and tossing ideas back and forth. No solution seemed quite to fit the need at hand until Henry Billings suggested a big Texas Hello in reverse.

'What exactly is a Texas Hello?' I asked.

'Not too sure,' he said. 'I may have made that up, but it fits whatever you call it. I think it originated from when a big Texas outfit hit an end of drive trail town.'

'Explain,' Surrette said.

'We get a mess of cattle together, maybe twenty head; beef is cheap at the moment and any reward should cover the outlay. One of us drives them hard and fast through the village and instead of being behind the cattle as expected, the rest of us will circle around and come in ahead of them, with a bit of luck and surprise, we can hit them from both ends but mostly from the direction they would least expect.'

'There's a reward?' I asked.

'New Mexico have put a price on the head of Sanchez. He's been a thorn in their side for some time and they would like to be rid of him, partly why we are here I suspect. It is election year and strange things do happen.'

Surrette said, 'You are damned right there, young man, and I like the idea of a Texas Hello, damned if I don't.'

And it was settled. Jardine was tasked with getting the small herd together and it was decided Charlie Moyes, being a cowhand before he was a Texas Ranger, and the smallest target among us, would drive them in.

As was often the case in desert places, the night was bitterly cold and the chill clung to us through the early dawn and into the mid-morning. With our help, Moyes pushed the newly-acquired cattle on at a fast rate, crossing the border just after noon, making the outskirts of the village by four o'clock. There we waited a half hour for Jardine and Surrette to catch up on their hired ponies, before separating to our various positions for the coming scrap. The good thing about the planned attack was that it required shooting from the backs of fast-moving horses, a skill all five of us had acquired at one time or another although, without a doubt, Wolf was the most accomplished in this, being a Comanche. He was more used to his Henry, but the marshal loaned him a .44.40 Colt Army similar to mine and familiar to him.

The cattle milled at one end of the street briefly before we heard a terrific scream from Wolf who had opted to ride with Moyes should he need covering fire. The bunched cattle took off at a run, spewing dust and shale in their wake, blotting out the sky. At that same time at our end of street, Surrette yelled, 'Let's get her done boys. . . .' and crouching low over the neck of his horse, led the charge and charge it was, cavalry all the way, lacking only the bugle call and a fluttering guidon. A county deputy, one elected county sheriff, a Texas Ranger and an over-the-hill town marshal, all on the charge, picking our targets from the disorientated defenders as they sought through the smoke and the dust to see where the enemy fire was coming from, only to discover too late, it came mostly from their rear. As they turned, Moyes and Wolf abandoned the cattle and were in the fight.

I swung down from the chestnut as we jumped a low wall, hitting the ground at a run and entering the backyards of a row of adobe buildings. Reins trailing, she stood firm, her long-ago training coming into play at the sound of gunfire. I slapped her hard on the rump with my hat, driving her from the line of battle. She ran and leapt back over the wall, stirrups flying. My horse first and God and country second, still all cavalry man at heart.

Colt in hand, I jumped over the next low wall and came under rifle fire from a building across the street. Several pistol shots rang out and the rifle fire ceased, and I watched as Henry Billings dashed from the building and crossed the dust-filled street, running low, crouched over. He leaped the wall, a big grin on his young face. I nodded my thanks and thumbed fresh rounds into the hot cylinder of my Colt.

'The others?' I asked.

'Around, they know where we are, just seen that old lawman standing out there in the street, emptying his gun then rolling across to the gully and cackling like a madman. Don't know where Wolf is at but heard a Henry just now, so I guess he ditched the handgun first chance he got. And you?'

'So far so good.'

I raised my head above the wall and a round took my hat clean off my head. I cursed, straightened briefly and emptied the pistol three rounds for each of the two windows and the shooting stopped. I turned to young Billings. 'You go right, and I'll head left for the cantina, it appears to be empty. When I get there, I'll run through and meet you out back.'

He scrabbled away and seconds later came back, tossing me my hat, with that endless grin on his face. 'Good job it wasn't a tight fit,' he said, and then he was gone.

Ducking low and after reloading, I quickly

moved from house to house, as we had planned around the table that morning, I headed in the direction of the cantina, passing several dead bodies as I went.

If there were civilians in the vicinity I did not see them and assumed they had fled when the bandits had made it clear to them that their village was to become the centre of a gunfight. I leaped over the last of the low adobe walls, stepped cautiously into the darkened room of the small cantina and rapidly moved to one side of the doorway so as not to be backlit by the late-setting sun.

Two men turned to face me, both as surprised to see me as I was to see them, and both were armed. The nearest man threw up his gun, and still moving, I fired from the hip, hitting him in the shoulder, spinning him hard around and against the wall. Dropping his gun, his back toward me, he settled there, a miserable sound coming from deep within his breast. The other man I recognized instantly as Jorge Emilio Palmas. He fired a wild round at me and made for the open back door. I was of a mind to let him run but for some reason he paused, turned and took another shot at me; this one tugged at the sleeve of my jacket so I put him down. He bounced off the door frame before falling out on to the hardpacked yard.

The first man I had shot was moaning low, he rolled over and stared up at me, his crooked lips moving but no words coming from them. There was no mistaking his identity. Miguel Sanchez, his ruined face a carved grimace. My shot back at the cabin all those months ago had left a dimple of a scar on his left cheek but had taken away half of his lower right jaw, leaving a deep, scarred hole of ugliness. I quite suddenly felt a twinge of unjustified compassion, thinking of what this man must have gone through in those long months. I lowered the hammer of the Colt and let it hang down by my side.

I looked again into the scarred face of the man I had hunted down, but I could not pull the trigger. A smile began to form on his ruined mouth, the lips twitched as I lowered the Colt and his hand groped feebly for his fallen revolver. Surrette, however, did not share my compassion. He stepped through the doorway, passed me by, raised his smoking revolver and shot the Comanchero in the head. I stared at him, open-mouthed but not sure of the words needed. He looked at me, a dark smile on his face. 'It will save on the paperwork is all. We should not be down here.' He turned on his heel and limping, made his way back to the open doorway.

'You hurt?' I asked, noting the blood on his pants.

He turned back towards me. 'Just a scratch, a ricochet I think. Third time, same damned leg, just seems to attract lead.' He looked at me long and hard. 'That bother you, what I did in there?'

'Surprised me a little maybe, but it did not overly bother me. I have seen such unpredictable and impulsive behaviour on the battlefield many times. Soldiers often get medals for it.'

'That was no impulse, son, that was for Jonas Coop, my dead deputy in Drago Wells. He was a fine, young man. I thought he might wear this badge someday when I quit. Now I wonder just where it will end up.'

I watched as Surrette went back out and into the suddenly-silent street, the only sound the distant bawling of frightened cattle, muted by the ringing in my ears. I had forgotten to protect my hearing. I lingered a moment then, holstering my weapon, I turned for the back door and went through to examine the condition of Jorge Emilio Palmas. Charlie Moyes was already there standing over the very dead man. He looked at me. 'You shoot him, Mr Luck?'

I nodded.

'Hit him dead centre. He the one Wolf told us was feared of wolverines?'

I nodded again.

'Damned fool Mex, there aren't no wolverines in Texas, everyone knows that.'

'Apparently, he did not,' I said, turning back inside and following Surrette's footsteps out to where Wolf, Jardine and Henry Billings had brought up our horses.

There were no civilian casualties, we were all unscathed, apart from the sheriff's creased leg and, miraculously, not a single animal, horse or cow had been injured. It happens like that sometimes. We left money with the village headman to bury the sixteen dead and to pay for a padre, if one could be found, and told him he could keep the unbranded cattle Jardine had spirited up from the Devil only knows where. The man was delighted. The beasts that had so noisily heralded our brief visit to his village were a gift well worth having.

Surrette mounted his hired pony with some difficulty and a great deal of cursing and the five men sat there waiting on me, Wolf holding the reins of my horse.

Surrette said quietly, 'Time to get back to Texas. Are you coming, Mr Luck?'

Back in Abbotsville the morning following the gunfight, a very happy Henry Billings and Charlie Moyes said their farewells and headed for Fort Worth and home. Jardine, Surrette, Wolf and I shared the last, quiet evening in the hotel bar together and the sheriff was gone by first light, leaving Wolf and I to follow at our leisure.

For me it was all over, and I was glad of it.

CHAPTER FIFTEEN

WHEN THE DAY IS DONE

We took the long, easy way back to Canterville. We rested our horses often and smoking cigarette or pipe, we nattered the long evenings away. Something had changed in Wolf and I wasn't too sure exactly how, why or what it was. It would be wrong to say he had become less Indian in his outlook, that was never going to happen. In spite of his background in Michigan, he was all Comanche. He was still cranky, and he was still a little distant, but that distance had shortened, had become less obvious over the past weeks. He had taken care of me twice, once when I was injured and once when I was on the bottle and hell-bent for self-destruction. Too simplistic to say he had become a father-figure to me; more accurately, he was more of an elder and trusted big brother. Sometimes it is destructive to delve too deeply into the meaning of a relationship, suffice to know that if it works it works, and the way it works is best left alone.

He hunted regularly, cooked fine meals over a camp fire and we ate well, the grub sweetened now and then from a bottle of wine, one of three Jardine had given me as a leaving gift.

I was almost sorry when we made trail's end and sat the hilltop overlooking Canterville. I heard the distant river and smelled the night smells, listened to a lone wolf hammering away at the near full moon and I did not want to ride down the hill and come face to face with the multiple decisions needed to form any sort of a meaningful future. I had buried them in the back of my mind and wanted them to stay there. Wolf rode up beside me. 'Lovely, Harry, a beautiful land, day or night, my land.' He moved forward but I held the chestnut's head firm.

He turned to me. 'Are you coming?'

'You go on ahead, Wolf, I will be along in a couple of days or so. I need a little more time out here in the peace and quiet to think things through is all.'

'Thinking's a good thing just so long as you don't think too much. I'll pick up some supplies on my way through town if your credit is still good.'

'It's still good.'

'OK then, see you in a day or two. Don't take too long, we've got cattle to brand. You remember the cattle, don't you?'

He waited for my answer. I nodded but he still waited, the buckskin fidgeting impatiently under him. 'Yes,' I said, 'I remember them, big noisy things that often smell bad. Tell them I'm on my way. I'll see you in a couple of days.'

'No stopping off in town for a drink or two of whiskey?'

'No, I promise,' I said, turning the horse's head back the way we had come.

He smiled, reassured and turned his animal's head toward Canterville. 'See you at the Horseshoe then.'

I rode and thought, conspired with nature, God and all outdoors but found no answers, it was hard to think beyond the next hour or the next day. When I had left Fort Laramie, I had a clear destination, a set of plans that, if adhered to, would give me a good and fulfilling life. But plans are just that, plans, intransient things with no meaning beyond one's own imagination and so easily disrupted. A Mexican bandit, a lovely woman, and a fire had each altered the course of those plans and forced me to think of either bending with the winds of change or starting anew. Five days and five nights and I was no nearer to reaching a decision than I was when Wolf had left me.

I gave up on trying and headed back for Canterville. It was early evening before I reached town for the second time and only moments ahead of a wind-driven, violent and noisy rain storm backed up by rolling thunder and sheet lightning. I put the horse in the livery and told the boy to rub her down and feed her. With that done, I pulled on my slicker and hurriedly crossed the already muddy street to George Surrette's office where a light was still burning.

I busted straight in and fought to close the wind-battered door behind me. Surrette looked up from the blown about newspaper he had been reading, removed his wire-rimmed eyeglasses and smiled broadly at me. 'About time you showed up. Wolf has been back near on a week. What kept you?'

'This and that,' was all I could come up with.

'You want a cold glass of wine? Henry just sent a bottle over.'

'Thanks, that would go down well.'

He poured two generous tin mugs of white wine and we toasted absent friends. 'I take it you have not been out to the Horseshoe, came straight here?'

'Yes,' I said. 'I needed to think things over, get my life back together. It's been a hell of a year, what with one thing and another. I'm tired of walking, running and riding. I'm weary of the sound of gunfire. That Mex village did it for me.'

'Do you know what they called that fracas down in New Mexico?'

I shook my head. 'They actually gave it a name?'

'The Gunfight at the Nameless Village, has kind of a ring to it don't you think.'

It wasn't really a question, so I let it pass.

'Sixteen Comancheros killed. The governors of both Territory and State were tickled pink. Election year, *mucho* kudos for Texas and New Mexico.' He paused, suddenly interested in his fingernails and then looked up at me. 'You will find a few changes out there at the ranch. Go home for a few days, take some time, see what pans out. You just never know in this life what's waiting around the next bend of the river.' He smiled knowingly. 'You just never know, Mr Luck.'

'I'll study on it some.'

'Well here's something else for you to think on. This is election year and I aim to quit and spend the rest of my days raising horses.'

I started to speak but he held up his hand.

'You are tailormade for this office. You stand tall round here, with my support you will get elected. You are a born lawman if there is such a man.'

'No way, George. I'm a rancher or maybe a soldier but not a lawman.'

'You haven't done a day's ranching in your whole life let alone your time here and you quit the army or maybe the army quit you. I was never sure on that.'

'Wrong,' I said. 'I have been invited to re-enlist with a raise in rank and I may do just that, go back to Laramie a major. I like the sound of it.'

'You just like the sound of your own voice. Anyways you think on it, you may well find something changes your mind. This is good country and no reason you can't run the Horseshoe and wear the county badge.' There was something odd in his rasping tone as if he were teasing me, as if he knew something I did not.

We shook hands and I unpinned the star and offered it back, but he waved it away. 'Keep it, at least for the time being. If you decide to run for office, it will look good on the vest of the winning candidate.'

I shook my head, slipped the badge into my shirt pocket, finished my drink and made for the hotel. It was not a night for riding. Me, a county sheriff, it seemed unlikely and I wondered what had made Surrette reach the conclusion that I could fill his boots. I oft-times wonder at the devious workings of the minds of men.

CHAPTER SIXTEEN

THE HOMECOMING

The storm blew itself out overnight and although the trail was muddied in places, the grass-covered High Plains drank the water like a thirsty animal. The Horseshoe below me was bathed in a pale, morning-mist shrouded glow as the warm air got to work on the moisture left by the dew that followed the rain. Smoke drifted out from the larger of the two stone chimneys and I caught a brief glimpse of Wolf as he made his way out to the pole corral. He stopped mid-stride and looked up the hill toward me for a very long moment and then waved before continuing his journey.

'How the hell could you see me from down here to way up there?' I asked as I unsaddled the chestnut and stacked the rig on the corral's top rail.

'Couldn't see you. Too far for these old eyes but I knew you were there, I'm a Comanche, remember? You go on up to the house, coffee is on the stove, breakfast will be ready directly.'

'OK, boss,' I said, with a smile.

I was maybe fifteen yards from the ranch house door when it opened and Bonnie Luxford ran out, her lemon-coloured dress seeming to fly her down the steps, leaped up at me, threw her arms around my neck and kissed me hard on the mouth. 'Where the hell have you been, Harry Luck? I'd almost given up, thought maybe you knew I was here and didn't want to see me.' She was laughing. I do not believe I have ever seen anyone so happy, so brimming with joy. I stared at her, stunned, my knees trembling, not knowing what to do so I did what comes naturally and pulled her to me and kissed her back.

We ate a quick breakfast and Wolf insisted he had work to do, smiled at me and left. Bonnie and I cleared the table, drank some more coffee and then sat hand in hand on the stoop's double-seated swing which had not been there when I left. 'Wolf made it for us,' she said. 'Old coot's a bit of a romantic at heart. He wrote me, you know, a while back now, back when you were. . . .'

'A drunk,' I finished it for her.

'Yes, then. He was very concerned for you. Did you know that?'

'It's very hard to know anything about Wolf,' I said.

'He told me about the letters you wrote me and never posted. I came out here to read them, after all they were addressed to me. Do you mind that I did?'

I could feel the tears of relief in my eyes. I hoped that she could not see them, but she did and, taking off the red bandanna that covered most of her hair, wiped them away. 'They were lovely letters filled with the things we would have talked about had I not been so narrow-minded. Do you forgive me for that? Do you want me to stay?'

'You are never going to leave the Horseshoe again,' I said, confidently adding, 'and neither am I.'

Just then, Wolf walked by leading his paint horse, heading up to the small cabin. He waved, smiled and walked on but did not look back. And I promised myself there and then that looking forward was the only truthful way for any man.

EPILOGUE

And that is my story, the story of Harry James Luck, Civil War veteran, US Cavalry captain, sometime lawman, gambler and one-time drunk.

Bonnie Luxford and I were married a month or so following the gunfight in which Miguel Sanchez and Jorge Emilio Palmas, along with fourteen of their comrades died at the so-called Gunfight at the Nameless Village. We have two children, a boy and a girl, Tobias and Harriet, and they enjoy our company as much as we do theirs. I ran for the office of county sheriff and, as Surrette had predicted, and with his support, got myself elected and there is talk of me running for higher office, but I must think long and hard about that. I like walking the Main Street of our growing community, behind the badge, knowing I have good deputies to back me and a successful ranch in the Horseshoe with Charlie Moyes as my top hand. He quit the Rangers to come and work for me and, I firmly believe, just to be near his idol, Wolf Keogh. Henry Billings is now a captain in the Rangers and his brother, a sergeant; they call into Canterville whenever in this part of the state.

George Surrette still runs his horse ranch just outside of Canterville. He visits with us often, either at Bonnie's town house or the Horseshoe. He is not as grumpy as he once was but is still feisty when it comes to talking about law and order and the State of Texas.

We heard that Ben Jardine resigned his job as Abbotsville's town marshal and went to live with his sister in Albuquerque, taking the ginger cat that masqueraded as a wolverine with him. He wrote us for a while and when the letters stopped we guessed he had, as all men must, run out his string.

Jack Pelham visited us just the one time and was pleased to see that the graves of his wife and children were cared for and flowered with paintbrush and bluebonnet, tended by Bonnie who also kept the Comanche graves in good order. Pelham looked fit and lean and had remarried but needed to see the graves one more time. He stayed two days, and on both occasions George Surrette was also a guest.

Wolf is gone and we know not where. He lived in the small cabin for several years, growing older and crankier. The children loved to sit and listen to his often bullshit stories as did I and, on occasion, did Bonnie. One morning he was gone. He left two unopened sacks of Bull Durham and his black hat with the eagle feather in the braided band on the kitchen table, but he did not leave a note, guessing I suppose, that I would know where he had gone. I finally retired my battered Stetson, beat some shape into his reservation headgear, and now wear that with both pride and Bonnie's wholehearted approval. I am not sure that I ever got to know the real Wolf Keogh but I miss him every day and sometimes at twilight, sitting on the porch of the little cabin, drawing on my evening pipe, I feel his presence, feel that he is somewhere close by and is still watching over us. That would be the Comanche way.